Strange Markings©

A Skylar Drake Mystery

by

Janet Elizabeth Lynn and Will Zeilinger

Strange Markings

A Skylar Drake Mystery

Copyright © 2015

Janet Elizabeth Lynn and Will Zeilinger

ISBN: 1519672643
ISBN-13: 978-1-51967264-3
Ebook ISBN: 978-1-311-83198-9E

Cover design by Those Designers

Printed in the United States of America

Dedication

To our family and friends for their support
and willingness to be part of this story,
we give a heartfelt, THANK YOU!

Acknowledgements

This novel never would have been completed without the support and guidance of many kind souls.

The Moloka'i Public Library provided much needed details about life on the island in the 1950's

Our mid fall trip to Honolulu to visit Keith and Peggy Zeilinger gave us wonderful ideas and in making the novel a true Polynesian flavor.

A special thank you goes to Leilani Frando, a lover of Spam, and Kristoffer Ferrer who brought the story to life with cultural information and extraordinary characters.

A special acknowledgement must go to the members of Sisters In Crime, Los Angeles chapter.

To our small family, without whom life would not be complete, we give our warmest thank you for the love and support they show us for each book.

Other Books by the Authors
Janet Elizabeth Lynn & Will Zeilinger
Skylar Drake Mystery Series
• Slivers of Glass

Janet Elizabeth Lynn
www.janetlynnauthor.com

Murder Mysteries
• South of the Pier
• West of the Pier
• East of the Pier
• North of the Pier
Cozy Mysteries
• Eggnog
• Charlotte Russe
• Crepes Suzette
Cookbooks
• Recipes from the novel
Eggnog Cookbook
• Recipes from the novel
Crepes Suzette Cookbook
• Recipes from the novel
Charlotte Russe Cookbook
• The Pier Mysteries Cookbook

Will Zeilinger
www.willzeilingerauthor.com

• The Naked Groom
• Something's Cooking at Dove Acres
• The Final Checkpoint
• Oh Dear! (cartoon book)
*A collection of funny thoughts
for Baby Boomers and Beyond*

Chapter One

I glanced out the rain speckled window of the streetcar as we crossed over the 11 Freeway heading west toward Wilshire. Nobody was going anywhere fast. It's 1955, the freeways were supposed to ease traffic and get us to our jobs quicker but it looked more like a parking lot out there.

The streetcar stopped to let off passengers. I glanced to my left and saw a green Ford pushed up over the curb, wrapped round a utility pole, front end badly smashed in. It looked like my partner Casey's car. I tore out of the streetcar and ran past another wrecked car to the corner.

"Did you see that maniac?" the driver shouted, "He slammed into the back of my car, backed up into the front of that one and took off."

Bev Dolan, Casey's ex, looked dazed as she was helped out of the wrecked car. Police cruisers began to show up. "Bev, you okay?" I looked inside, "Is Casey all right?" but he wasn't there. The car was a write-off. "What happened?"

She held her lower lip, blood all over her hand and chin.

Bev and I never got along. But ever since she married my best friend, we tolerated each other.

"Excuse me." A young woman appeared, "What can I do? I'm a nurse." We helped Bev to the sidewalk and sat her down. "Sir," the nurse asked, "do you have a clean handkerchief?"

I handed her mine. "Hold this on your lip, Ma'am and press." She proceeded to examine Bev's head, "Good, no bleeding. Did you hit your head too?"

Bev shook her head and muttered, "Just my face." We could smell bourbon on her breath. I looked at my watch, only 8:30 in the morning.

A couple of officers came over to take Bev's statement. I took them aside, "Apparently a car pushed the first car over the tracks. When the streetcar approached, they backed up and slammed into the green car, pushing her into the utility pole, then sped off." They nodded and took notes.

"Looks like it might have been an attempted gang hit," I told the officer.

When he looked up from his notes our eyes met, it was Graves, a former supervisor who was demoted after the inquest into Claire and Ellie's death in the house fire. I still haven't forgiven the clown. He chose to ignore me and continued to interview the witnesses. The young nurse waved an ambulance over to tend to Bev.

"Did you see what happened?" Graves asked the nurse.

She nodded.

"Did you get the license plate number off the car that fled?"

She shook her head no.

"Why the hell not?"

A typical response for Graves, no wonder he was demoted.

He shook his pencil in her face, "You see an accident, you get the license plate number." The nurse was near tears, but Graves pushed it, "...typical female logic."

"Hey, back off you..." I wasn't going to let him get

away with that, "There are ladies present and that one is trying to help."

The nurse was a bleached blond, pretty and efficient. She smiled and tilted her head, "What about you sir? Are you okay?" She had kind eyes.

"Thanks, but I wasn't involved." I headed to Bev as they walked her to the ambulance. "Where's Casey?"

"He's busy working that assignment you gave him so he let me use his car."

We watched a tow truck wrench the mangled Ford off the pole. An officer turned to us, "We'll take it down to the impound yard,"

"I won't be able to reach Casey until he gets back to our office," I told Bev. "I took the streetcar, so I can't drive you home from the hospital."

"I'll call a neighbor."

I looked around for the nurse to thank her but she was gone. A real Florence Nightingale.

~~~~~~~~~~

I had hoped for some relief from the hot, rainy weather in the air conditioned offices of Steele Investigations, but when I pulled open the lobby doors of the old building, I was met by darkness. Hot, stale, humid darkness. No one was at the reception desk. I turned toward the elevator door. "Out of Order" was scrawled on a sheet of paper and taped to the doors. The power was out and that meant no lights, elevator, or air conditioning. Steele had leased his office in a building built before the Depression and it demonstrated its advanced age. This was turning out to be a crappy day.

In the dark, I dug a pen light out of my trouser pocket

and trudged up to the fourth floor. Through the frosted glass office door I could see daylight from the windows. When I pushed the door open, mail was piled on the floor right beneath the mail slot and the place smelled like a damp cellar. Miss Little, Steele's obnoxious secretary, decided she couldn't work with Dolan and me when we took over the company after Mike got sent away for tax evasion. We decided not to hire a replacement yet, and the last four months have gone smoothly without one.

I looked at the desk. Casey had left a note scribbled on a steno pad, *Drake, I'll be late. Telephone not working.* Could this day get any worse? No phone meant no business. I unbuttoned the top couple of buttons on my shirt and thumbed through the mail. Casey's turn to handle the bills, so I tossed them on the left side of the desk. Three envelopes got my attention. I slit them open and saw that both lawyers had sent me an update on my pending court cases. Oscar Lane said he was still waiting for a court date on the LAPD suit for the wrongful death of my wife and daughter. I felt the anger all over again as I wadded it up and tossed it in the wastepaper basket. The second was from Leland Morehead. He was ready to file a suit against Prestigious Studios for blacklisting me as a stunt man. He listed it as "restriction of trade." I've worked too long and put myself in danger too many times to be ignored. They thought I'd just go away when they dumped me like yesterday's newspaper. "This is going to take a long time," I mumbled, "I'm fed up with being treated like a dog by those suits at the studio." I'll tell Morehead to go ahead and picked up the phone. Nothing. Crap! I forgot...phones out. I gotta go down and call from the pay phone on the corner. I left that letter on the desk and opened the third with "RD Talent Agency" on the return address. I wondered what Ricky Dicky wanted.

> *Mr. Drake,*
>
> *As your publicist, I am taking on an associate, Mitch Cline. He will be assisting me with my growing list of prestigious clientele. Rest assured your account will not change and you will be well taken care of. I will continue to be part of the company. Call me if you have any questions.*
> *RD*

So Ricky got himself an assistant. He was accustomed to making a small mint off of my local TV show, which was now on hold. Dicky better keep working for me or I'll find a different agent when we start up again.

I cranked opened the blinds and lifted the sash of the fourth floor window. Ah, fresh air. Below, people strolled by and cars scurried around like busy ants with horns honking and tires screeching. The Red Pacific Electric street car buzzed by. I took in a deep breath and looked toward the coast. I'd bet it was a lot cooler on the beach.

When I pulled my head inside, I heard the door to the outer office open and close.

"Just a minute," I yelled as I went around the desk and fixed my tie in the wall mirror. When I opened the door, a woman with carrot red hair and big green eyes stood by the receptionist desk holding a small handkerchief to her nose. She was kind of pretty in a Technicolor way. Sweat beaded on her freckled forehead and neck.

"Gee whiz. Are you trying to save money on the

utilities or something? I could barely find your office in the dark and it's stifling in here."

"I'm really sorry, Miss, power's out. Would you like some water?"

She shook her head, "No thank you, I'd like to speak to a..." She read from a business card, "Mr. Steele, please."

"Sorry, Ma'am, he's not here... Mr. Steele's on a sabbatical for about eight years. My name's Drake, Skylar Drake, Private Investigator." I ushered her into my office where the window was open. Her high heels clicked on the worn hardwood floors as I followed her inside. She waited for me to pull a chair over to the desk. After she swiped at it with her handkerchief, she sat down, I handed her my business card and tried, unsuccessfully, not to stare at those legs!

She tucked the card in her purse and pulled off her gloves. "I'm Loretta Carrington." She looked around the office with a look of disgust. "Apparently my Aunt Marion spoke with Mr. Steele a year ago or so. I've come here at her request."

I sat forward and took a pad and pencil out of the desk. There was something sexy about her alabaster skin, the sprinkle of freckles on her cheeks, and her legs. The way she held herself said old money.

She daintily dabbed the sweat on her neck with her handkerchief, "My Uncle moved to Hawaii about twenty years ago and married a native girl. He kept in contact with my aunt for years, well... until eighteen years ago when we were notified that he, along with his wife and daughter, died in a car accident in the hills above Honolulu. Their remains weren't discovered until several days later. After a

12

while we learned their four year-old son, my cousin, had roamed the hills alone before anyone noticed he was missing and called the police. After they found him, Chewy was sent to live with us."

"Chewy?"

She smiled, a beautiful smile, "That's his nickname. His given name is Otis Carrington. Aunt Marion took Chewy in and raised the three of us." She paused. "When Chewy was eighteen he decided to move back to Hawaii. Aunt Marion insisted that he wait until he was twenty and had some college. But he refused and left."

"Three of you?"

"And my other cousin, Cassandra."

She fanned herself with her gloves, "Could I trouble you for that glass of water? It's so stifling hot." I got a couple of glasses and poured from the water cooler. When I handed her the glass, I detected the faint scent of lavender. My wife always wore that scent. The water felt good in my dry throat.

Miss Carrington took a long drink then sighed, "Mr. Drake, Chewy sent us a letter every month without fail. About a year ago things changed. His letters became shorter and sporadic. Then they stopped altogether. That's when Aunt Marion came to see Mr. Steele. She is worried sick. Nothing has changed, so she sent me to talk to you...Mr. Drake."

"And what would you and your Aunt want from me?"

"You're a former Los Angeles Police officer, right? Mr. Steele spoke highly of you."

"That's former Los Angeles Police *Detective*, yes."

13

"I'd like you to come to the house and speak with my Aunt Marion. She's quite elderly and in a wheelchair. It's difficult for her to get around now." She dug into her purse and pulled out a calling card. "Please... she's very worried and doesn't feel comfortable discussing this by telephone." Miss Carrington held it between her fingers and laid it in the palm of my hand.

I was floored when I saw the Bel Air address. It took a moment to absorb. I gathered my senses and looked her in the eyes, "Normally I don't make house calls, however, since your Aunt is frail and unable to travel, I'll make an exception." Since I'd never been inside the gates of Bel Air, I tried to justify going there.

"You will be compensated for your time, of course."

I scotch taped the card to my calendar, "Sure why not? How does tomorrow at 11am sound?"

She stood, "Thank you. Aunt Marion will be happy to hear that." When she turned to leave, my senses were filled with her lavender perfume again. I shut the door behind her and closed my eyes.

~~~~~~~~~~

Casey Dolan strode in. I knew it was him by the way his shoes slapped when he walked. He plopped down on the soft chair across the room and loosened his tie, "You find anything out about the lights and air conditioning Sky? I'm hot, dog tired and so glad I never had kids."

I'd given him the job Mike Steele wanted me to do. Basically it was babysitting some rich record producer's nineteen year-old daughter and her jewels. I called her a USC student with a PhD *Papa has dough* which meant a bottomless expense account. Her father was out of the

14

country for six months and hired us to keep watch on her and her baubles. She seemed to have a taste for bad boys. He was afraid her freeloading friends would take advantage of her. And without adult supervision the goodies would disappear. Casey was the perfect man for the job.

"Three more months of this and I'm FREE!"

"That bad, huh?"

He rolled his eyes. "You couldn't imagine."

"But it's very good money, and we need it, right?" I pointed to the stack of bills.

"Ah, that my friend is the pot o' gold at the end of this nightmare rainbow."

While he was in a good mood, I told him about Bev and the car accident. He grabbed the phone and slammed it back down. "Shit. I forgot the phone was out."

"Bev said she'll call her neighbor to pick her up. She'll be okay. Your car is another matter."

"I should have known better than to lend it to her. I'll get down to the impound yard so I can get it repaired." He picked up his hat and turned toward the door.

"I wouldn't bother Casey, it looked totaled to me."

He sat back down and put his head between his knees. After a couple of moments, he sighed and sat up, "Let's get some lunch." He pointed his finger at me, "Someplace with air conditioning. I'll call the hospital from there."

I put the letter opener in my desk drawer and closed the window. "I know just the place. Follow me."

Just as we opened the outer door to the hallway, two men in matching gray suits appeared outside the office, "We're looking for a Mr. Skylar Drake. Is he here?"

Chapter Two

The two men looked directly at me. "I'm Drake. Can I help you?"

Dolan stood right behind me.

"I'm Agent Miller, this is Agent Tanner." They flashed their badges, "We want to talk to you Mr. Drake." Miller looked past me and frowned at Dolan.

"I'll just wait out..." Casey moved toward the door.

I put my hand on Casey's shoulder. "This is my partner Casey Dolan, anything you have to say to me you can say to him."

They shrugged and stepped inside. "Let's go in your office." I showed them inside, as sweltering as it was.

Miller put his hat on top of the file cabinet. Tanner kept his on.

"We are investigating the disappearance of a Mr. Ted Stone. You're a known associate of his. Is this true?"

"Sure, I know Teddy. We worked on a few films together." I sat back in my chair while Casey stood by the door, "His sister Florence and I used to do stunts for Prestigious Studios a while back. Teddy started about a year later... you say he's missing?"

"His sister reported him missing a year ago. Our records show you were one of the last people to see him before he disappeared."

"You said a year ago?" I thought for a moment, "Yeah, that sounds about right. It was a war movie. There was a battle scene and we had to fall out some windows and off a moving truck like we'd been shot, y'know. This was

16

before..." I stopped myself. They didn't need to know about my law suit with the studio brass.

"Before what?" Agent Tanner asked.

"Before my last stunt gig with Flo."

"And the victim?"

"Victim? I thought you said he was missing."

"Just tell us about your last job."

"Well, Teddy and I shared a dressing room. It was about midnight when we finished the night scenes. After we changed and dropped our costumes off at wardrobe, we left for breakfast. That was about two in the morning. I took the bus home, and I guess he drove. I never saw him again after that. Flo and I did a shoot at the studio the following month. She told me she was going to Washington to get married. That was that."

The two agents took notes on everything I said.

Casey spoke up, "Do you mind if I ask what prompted this recent investigation?"

Miller put his pencil in his ear, "We found a man's remains in the Arizona desert. Our medical people said he was buried for about a year, so we only have bones, clothes, few personal items and his wallet. There was nothing in it except for his SAG membership card." He paused, "The Union said you worked with him. We found you in the phone book."

Agent Tanner pulled a cellophane envelope out of his pocket containing the card. There was Teddy, staring back at me. "Yes, that's Teddy and that is what he looks like." I showed it to Casey. He took a look and handed it back to Tanner.

"We're unable to locate his sister, do you know her married name?"

I thought hard, "I don't believe she told me. No. She never mentioned it. Flo just said she was leaving the business to get married and move to Washington."

"The remains are at the LA County Coroner's office. Since we can't locate next of kin, we'd like you to stop by and ID what you can."

I looked at Dolan. "What do you think?" He nodded.

~~~~~~~~~

We met them at the Coroner's office and waited for the Medical Examiner to get back from lunch. Casey called the hospital, Bev had gone home. He called his house, no answer. "I'm not worried," he said. His eyes said otherwise.

I hadn't been down here in a long time. Yep, the same frigid air, smell of alcohol and bleach have never left my mind. The door swung open and Dr. Harold Logue came in wiping his mouth with a paper towel. I remember he always ate at the most inopportune times, "Hey Drake and Dolan, LAPD's two best detectives. Nice to see both of you." Logue was an old timer. We worked a lot of cases with him. He put his arms on our shoulders, "Sure miss working with you two geniuses. I could never figure out how you caught all the bad guys. These youngsters they got in here now are..." He stopped when he saw the young FBI agents standing by the wall. "Oops, sorry. No offense," and shook their hands.

Agent Miller kept hold of Dr. Logue's hand, "We're here to see the remains of Ted Stone."

"Yes sure, come this way," Logue said.

He had the bones laid out on the table, a complete skeleton. How was I supposed to ID the remains of Teddy from this?

"I don't know if this will help you," Agent Tanner said, "but here are the clothes we found, his accessories and wallet."

The clothes looked like his. I knew him as a rather classy dresser when he wasn't working.

"We found a hundred dollar bill hidden in the wallet." Miller remarked

"You can't trace the bill?"

He shook his head, "We tried, nothing."

I knew Teddy well enough to know he didn't carry so much cash around. "He was a Las Vegas hound. We'd get paid. He'd go to Vegas and blow the wad, all of it - then come back broke. He was a real gambler and big with the ladies. I'm not surprised he had that much cash, but he seldom carried it around. He either banked it or lost it."

"And the clothes?" Agent Miller lifted his pencil from his notepad to point at the clothing spread on a different table. Dolan and I spent time looking at what they found. "Shirt, tie, suit, vest, socks, pants. It was all there."

"What about these?" Tanner asked.

On the counter was an assortment of gaudy men's rings, a tie bar, gold cuff links, bracelets and a watch. We knew not to touch them. It looked like his stuff, but something didn't seem right. I took another look at the clothes and jewels, but couldn't put my finger on it.

I straightened up, "Seems like his stuff. It's been a while."

19

"How do you think he died?" Dolan asked Logue.

"You knew him Mr. Dolan?" Miller asked.

Casey crossed his arms and shook his head, "No, we never met."

Dr. Logue picked up the skull. "Looks like he was hit in the head with a dull object. There are also a number of fractured ribs. I think he was beaten before being bludgeoned."

"Sorry Drake," Agent Tanner said, "but we have to ask, where were you last summer?"

Wait a second, did they think I had something to do with Teddy's disappearance?

"You'll have to be more specific," Dolan said. "Part of the summer both of us were on a special assignment in Santa Rosa in conjunction with the LAPD and Santa Rosa PD."

Miller looked up from his pad, "This can be verified?"

Most of the people who could verify our presence in Santa Rosa were in witness protection, prison or dead. "Olivia Jahns out of the San Francisco bureau can vouch for our work in Santa Rosa.

"Yes, we know her. Great agent." Tanner replied, "We'll check on that."

Miller and Tanner were already in the hallway when a light bulb went on in my brain, "Wait, I need to check something again."

I went back inside with the other three in tow and looked at the clothes. "These are not Ted's clothes. He never would have worn these."

"How do you know?" Miller looked at his watch.

"Ted Stone never wore such a plain business suit. He

20

wore tweed or pin stripes, never plain Jane stuff like this. And look. That's a white shirt, Ted was a blue or gray shirt guy." I moved to the counter and put on a pair of rubber gloves to pick up the cuff links. "Are these real rubies?"

Tanner shook his head, "No."

"What about the other stones?"

"Nope and the tie tack and bracelets are all cheap gold plate."

I tossed the cuff links onto the counter, "This isn't Teddy. He wouldn't be caught dead wearing this crap. Only the real McCoy for him. He had a reputation in Vegas. He needed them for insurance when he ran out of folding money."

Tanner and Miller scribbled some more notes as I referred them to the jeweler in Pasadena that Teddy used.

"Could he have hit a rough patch, pawned the real jewels and substituted fakes?"

"No, never. At least not a year ago. Last time I saw him he was loaded with cash."

"Well," Tanner asked, "Who the hell is this guy?"

I hated to leave the cool, dead quiet of the Coroner's office but Casey and I were starving. We headed for lunch

The front doors were wide open when we arrived at Clifton's Cafeteria. It looked like their air conditioner wasn't working either. It was miserably hot, but we were hungry.

We got our food and sat quietly sweating for some time. "So where is Ted Stone?" Dolan asked. "And who's the poor unfortunate fella on the table back there?"

"Maybe Teddy owed gambling debts. He could've

skipped town and left a dead body for the gangsters to find in his place." I swallowed half my glass of ice tea, "Well, whoever that was, doesn't concern me or my business."

Casey glared, "I do hope you'll be more concerned about me if I ever go missing." and took a big bite of his corned beef sandwich.

While he was chewing, I told him about my appointment in Bel Air with the Carrington family and the search for the missing relative. Casey set his sandwich down and took a drink of lemonade. "Now that, my boy, is some serious money. It's old money."

"I know. You should've seen the doll they sent over. I'm going up to their house in Bel Air to speak with the old lady."

"So, you get to go to a Bel Air mansion and I'm stuck with a spoiled child."

"Only three more months Casey, three more months."

We dropped in at Leland Morehead's law firm. Their air conditioner worked just fine.

When I introduced Leland to him, Casey held out his hand, "Always a pleasure to meet a solicitor."

As always, his Irish brogue shined brightly.

Morehead looked over my file, "Looks like you have a good case here, Mr. Drake. Prestigious Studios has no record of disciplinary action against you and in two months the Union will be firmly in place and rules in forced. I suggest you bide your time for a couple more months before filing this suit. Get the Union to help you on this."

"Is that good news?"

He sat back and patted the desk blotter, "You bet. The Studio does not want bad publicity. Plus, the union would like to win a case right up front to show they mean business. If need be, they can make a lot of noise in the media." He pointed his finger at me, "But... remember, those studio guys are known to get real nasty."

Noise? Not sure what he meant by that but I agreed, "Okay, if it works."

"It's better to try and get a little something over a lot of nothing."

Morehead had a point.

On the way back to the office, I described the Carrington woman who came to see me. Our two seats on the Pacific Electric streetcar were set on the side and perfect for a private conversation. I noticed that Casey seemed distracted.

"Okay, what's up?"

He turned his head slightly to the right, "Don't look, but you know that feeling you get when you're being tailed?"

I avoided turning my head to look. "Why?"

"Just keep sharp," he whispered, "Two men at the other end of the car have been following us from your solicitor's office."

I stood to adjust my pant legs and glanced to the right, two guys in hats on this sweaty summer day."

~~~~~~~~~

That night the TV news reported Bev's car accident. The camera man panned to everyone around the cars and the rails. I smiled as they showed me in deep conversation with Officer Graves and that nurse. I hope someone sees her or she sees herself and comes forward. She jumped right in and should get credit for her assistance.

Chapter Three

The drive up Beverly Glen Drive and across Sunset was slow going. I had to take a couple of detours because of flooded streets and that made me late for my appointment in Bel Air. I checked my watch as I arrived at the sprawling Carrington Estate. Century old trees surrounded the main house. Yellow yarn tied around a few of the old eucalyptus warned of possible falling limbs. A white wrought iron gate opened onto the circular drive. I parked away from the trees and stepped onto the mushy ground. My shoes squeaked and squished up the marble steps to the front door. I was surprised when the door wasn't answered by a butler or maid. It was Loretta Carrington, even prettier than at my office. "Nice to see you again, Mr. Drake, come in." I wiped my feet on the mat and stepped inside the spacious foyer. The shiny marble floors and tall windows all said money and power. She directed me to a set of huge white doors that opened to reveal a space enclosed by ceiling to floor windows. "This is our sun room. Please have a seat while I fetch my aunt."

This room reminded me of the Beverly Hills Hotel. The walls were painted lemon yellow. Sofas and chairs were upholstered in green and yellow stripes. The wrought iron chairs were painted white. It was all quite sterile looking. I was afraid to touch anything.

Just as I sat down, the doors opened and Loretta pushed a wheelchair carrying a thin, silvery haired woman into the room. Dressed in black, she sat poised as straight as a tree. Behind them, a dark haired woman followed wearing an eye popping floral bikini with a small robe over her arm.

The woman in the wheelchair held out her hand, turned downward for me, I guess, expecting me to kiss it. "Mr. Drake I presume?"

I rose, "Yes Ma'am," and shook her hand.

"I had expected to speak with Mr. Steele but Loretta tells me that he is unavailable for some time." She scowled up at her niece, "Well Loretta, introduce me properly and watch your manners."

That seemed a bit odd to say to a woman who appeared to be about twenty-five.

"Aunt Marion," Loretta extended her hand toward me, "Allow me to introduce Mr. Skylar Drake," I could tell she was tired from muscling the wheelchair in here. "Mr. Drake, Marion Carrington, my aunt, and my cousin Cassandra Carrington."

The dark haired beauty eyed me like a hungry cat. Cassandra's eyes never left mine while she put a cigarette between her lips. When I tried to turn my attention back to her Aunt, Cassandra took a small gold lighter from her cleavage, lit the cigarette, and blew a smoke ring in my direction.

"Well Mr. Drake?" Marion Carrington attempted to get the meeting back on track.

"Oh, yes. Nice to meet you, Ladies," I nodded and remained standing.

"Don't be so formal," Cassandra said. "Take a load off."

"Sandy!" Marion snapped, "Manners please!"

I chose one of the white wrought iron chairs.

Marion rolled her eyes and said, "I don't know what Lory told you or how correctly she relayed the information." While Loretta stood dutiful by the wheelchair, legs and all, Marion repeated exactly what Loretta told me at the office.

"Any idea where Otis, er... Chewy is now?" I asked.

"For God's sakes Drake, if we knew that, we sure wouldn't need you." Cassandra snapped, "Would we Auntie?" The way she was stuffed into that bikini made it hard to keep my eyes off her creamy curves.

"Sandy," Marion shouted, "Behave and cover yourself up." She shook her head in frustration and looked at me, "Now Mr. Drake, how should we begin?"

Sandy stubbed out her cigarette in an ash tray and tossed the short robe she'd had over her arm across her shoulders, though it didn't do much to cover her assets.

Marion turned her face toward me, "Mr. Drake, allow me to tell you about my nephew. Otis is sweet. He has a kind soul and big heart. He never felt sorry for himself, never asked why his parents died. Never."

"He had every right to ask that, too," Cassandra said.

Marion put her hand out to Loretta who handed her a lace edged handkerchief, "When Otis turned eighteen," Marion sobbed, "he insisted on going back to Hawaii to find himself. Apparently we weren't enough family for him."

"I knew he wouldn't come back." Cassandra lit another cigarette.

"He used to read about Hawaiian history and loved

27

pineapple," Loretta added.

"Mr. Drake, we haven't heard from him for over a year." Marion snapped her fingers. Loretta handed me a cardboard box. "Those are the last several letters I received."

I thumbed through the stack, taking note of the postmarks, "Is there anything else? Does he have a friend I could talk to?"

Marion shook her head and dabbed at the tears on her face, "He kept to himself at school."

"He was friendly to everyone," Cassandra added, "but no real friends, and no girlfriends...uh uh."

"You know," Loretta said, "He was close to Mr. Withers. They seemed to hit it off. He'd take Chewy fishing and to baseball games, you know like an uncle or big brother would do."

"Who's Mr. Withers? Was he one of the teachers?"

"No, James Withers is my accountant and family attorney. More importantly, he's an old family friend. I'll provide you with his business address and telephone number." Marion snapped her fingers again.

Loretta was already flipping through the telephone directory.

"Would there be anything else you need before you start work, Mr. Drake?" She wasn't asking a question.

"Thanks Ma'am, but I haven't decided to take the case yet. I'll have my staff look these over and I'll get back to you."

Loretta gave me a look that meant she knew I was a small operation and probably didn't have a staff. Especially after her visit to my office. Not exactly the best first

28

impression, I'll bet. I found a photograph of a brown faced teenager with straight black hair smiling back at me. I held it up and took a closer look at the photo "Is this Otis?"

Marion put her handkerchief down and looked. She nodded and sobbed some more.

"Does he have any tattoos or birth marks?"

"He has a line of small dark moles that ran across his left bicep," Cassandra said.

"But no tattoos?"

"Mr. Drake, I would never allow my nephew to deface his beautiful body in that manner." I got the impression I'd insulted her by asking. I slipped the photo back and closed the box. "As for the moles on his arm - well, they were from God."

"Thanks, the photo is a great help." I shook Marion Carrington's hand. "I'll be in touch in a couple of days."

Loretta walked me to the door. I took a look outside. It had stopped raining. She handed me a piece of stationary with the Carrington name embossed on top. "Here is Mr. Wither's telephone number and address. Perhaps he can give you more information about Chewy." She looked at her watch, "Oh, it's almost lunch time. I'd like to talk to you some more. May I meet you somewhere?"

"How about Greenblatt's Deli on Sunset?"

She glanced at her watch again, "In about twenty minutes then?"

I kept my head down to avoid stepping in a mud hole on the way back to my car. When I reached for the door, Cassandra came around from the other side of my car with a cigarette dangling from her lips. She'd let her trench coat fall open revealing the fact she was still sort of wearing that little bikini. Somehow I didn't notice that she vanished from the sun room while I was speaking to Marion.

"Uh, Miss..." I motioned her away from my car.

She took a puff and blew a smoke ring to my right. The breeze carried it way.

"Y'know, smoking is bad for your health." I gave her a look up and down, and she ate it up. "It'll stunt your growth."

She blew another puff my way.

"Do you mind? I need to go..."

"Don't take this case, Mr. Drake." she blurted.

"And why not?"

"Look, Chewy's a big boy now, an adult. If he chose to make a life for himself out of the clutches of that old biddy, no one should stop him. Leave him alone. He's happy. Don't screw it up for him."

"You sound like you know something that you're not telling me."

She took another drag and flicked the cigarette into the mud. "Just leave Chewy alone." She blew a last cloud of smoke at me and walked off with her hands in her pockets. I couldn't tell if she knew something about his disappearance or had something to do with it.

I waited for the Carrington girl at Greenblatt's when I heard the bell over the door jingle. I put down my cherry Coke and turned to see Loretta silhouetted against the harsh light of the doorway. She took off her gloves and sunglasses, and slid into the booth across from me. "Sorry I'm late." The aroma of lavender enveloped her. Even over

30

the smell of onions, cold cuts, and vinegar, her delicate floral scent made my head swim. She raised her eyes from the menu. They were beautiful, the same color as Claire's. "Do you see anything you like?" she asked.

"What?"

"I was asking what you usually order for lunch." She closed her menu. "Are you all right Mr. Drake?"

I cleared my head and answered, "Ahem, uh... cold tongue sandwich on rye with hot mustard... and potato salad." She shook her head, "Oh my, I don't think my digestive system could handle that." She flipped the menu open again as the waiter approached, "I think I'll have a chicken salad sandwich on dry white toast... and a few sliced tomatoes on the side." She handed her menu to the waiter and wiped her hands with her napkin while I ordered."

After he walked away, she leaned close, "I saw you speaking with Sandy next to your car."

I sipped my coke and nodded, trying to avoid getting lost in her eyes again.

"Look," she whispered, "I know something must've happened to Chewy. Auntie loved him with all her heart and he loved her. It's not like him to not communicate with her."

"When you say communicate, do you mean write?"

She nodded, "He also called a few times in the last two years. He couldn't afford the long distance calls, so he'd call collect. But he only did that if he hadn't written for a while so Aunt Marion wouldn't worry.

"Why does Sandy think there's nothing to

31

investigate?"

She shook her head, "She doesn't want to lose her inheritance. If Auntie spends a lot of money on a detective, she thinks it will mean less for her in the end."

The waiter arrived with our lunch.

"Do you think Cassa.. er, Sandy had something to do with his disappearance?"

Loretta thought for a moment, "No. They were very, very close."

She paused and took a breath... I felt she wanted to say more, "Mr. Drake, please take this case. It kills me to see my Auntie so upset and lost. She needs to know what's happened to Chewy. Whatever the outcome, it would be better than not knowing. Even if he's moved, she'd be content with knowing he was okay."

I leaned back and looked away so I could think.

"Miss Carrington, may I call you Loretta?"

"Please call me Lory."

"Fine, Lory. If Chewy is in the Hawaiian Islands and I have to go there, that would mean I'd have to leave my business here. I'm not sure if..."

"But, can't your partner take care of things while you're away?"

She'd been checking up on me. I loosened the top button of my shirt, "It's complicated."

"Please!" she interrupted and put her hand on mine. "If it's the money, don't worry about it. We can pay whatever you need. I beg you Mr. Drake. Please find Chewy."

I pulled my hand away, "Okay, I'll talk to my partner and see if he..."

"No! We want you Mr. Drake...you."

32

"Why? My partner Casey Dolan is an excellent detective, highly respected at the Police Department."

"Mr. Steele recommended you and it's you we want."

"So Mike recommended me?" I had trouble believing he'd do anything that would cut into his piece of the pie. "When was this?"

"When Auntie went to see him. He said that he'd put his best detective on it and named you."

I was his only detective, but I just nodded.

"Listen Miss Carrington..."

"Lory, please."

"Okay Lory, I need to line up a few things before I can give a green light to this case. Wait for my call before you say anything to your aunt." We finished and I walked her to her car.

She held my arm and pleaded with her eyes. This whole thing was killing me.

"I'll call you in the next two days. Promise."

That comment got me a slight smile, "Okay, Mr. Drake. I'll be waiting to hear from you!"

<u>Chapter Four</u>

I drove over and picked up Casey. He wanted to see his car and it was locked up in the LAPD impound lot.

As we entered the lobby, Captain Robb happened to be walking out. He asked both of us to stop by his office afterward. I didn't want to, but Dolan said, "Sure, no problem."

"I don't like this Casey," I whispered.

"What's it going to hurt to find out what he wants?"

His Ford looked worse than it did on the street.

"Like I said, Casey my boy, it's totaled."

He scratched his head, "Mother of all saints! I can't fix this wreck, it would take too much money. It'd be cheaper to buy another one."

"What kind?"

His eyes twinkled, "You seen the '55 Chevy Corvette? They've been out a couple of years now. Maybe the price has come down."

I shoved him with my elbow, "No way Buddy. You'd have to hock your house and live in your car."

He jammed his hands in his pockets, "Maybe a brand new Ford Thunderbird. Have you seen those? They come with a V8."

Considering his ex-wife had caused this mess, I thought he was taking it very well. "You and Bev back together?"

"Nah, just a trial run at seeing each other. Besides,

since she got evicted I'm letting her stay at my place for a couple of weeks. After that she's out."

"You got car insurance? It was a hit and run," I reminded him.

"Nah, never saw the need to spend good money on that old car."

~~~~~~~~~~

I guess I was still poison around here. Everyone in the Precinct chose to ignore me and it seemed to have rubbed off on Dolan. My lawsuit against the department made my name mud to most everyone here.

Robb ushered us into his office. It had been repainted and finally got some new blinds.

"Looks good," I said. "Has a nice cleaner feel to it than I remember."

"Shut up," he moaned. "I don't like doing this but have no choice."

"Doing what?"

Dolan looked at me, "Kisses of Santa Rosa?"

"Do you mean it smacks of Santa Rosa?" Robb asked. "Your Irish sometimes gets the better of your American English."

Robb stared at Casey for a moment, "I'm expecting to fill the Commissioner vacancy. I need a replacement for my spot, immediately." He paused and now looked at me. "There are two dead men in my morgue right now and I need independent consultants to work on this. I've instructed my successor to keep an eye on you." He buzzed his phone, "Now," Robb yelled into the box.

A young, college looking guy, entered. "Lieutenant

Nelson," Robb said, "These are the Bobsey Twins I told you about."

He straightened his lapels, shot his cuffs and held out his hand, "Glad to meet you, Paul Nelson." He had close set eyes. His big smile was the kind I didn't trust."

"I'm late for another appointment," Captain Robb stood, "Nelson will explain the whole sordid mess to you."

Without a word, we followed Nelson directly to the morgue. He knew we didn't need a guided tour.

Bodies of two adult males laid on the tables. Straight black hair, tanned and muscular. They looked like swimmers or surfers. The Medical Examiner, Dr. Logue saw us and socked us each in the arm, "Wow, you guys are back already. Things were getting a bit dull around here." He went on to explain that both men had been dead for about two days. The men looked 18 or 20 years old, brown skinned and tattooed with strange markings...flames maybe?" He pointed to one of the bodies, "They found this one in San Pedro. He was killed during a parade. The second body was found in Torrance. Same tattoos as the first - and the same MO. No identification, just big guys with tattoos. We're still trying to figure out what killed them. It looks like they were shot by the same type of weapon, but no shell casings were recovered at either scene. They were found about ten miles apart."

"So what killed them?"

"Looks like they were both shot in the upper back with some kind of a gun.

Along with the tattoos, both had similar moles on their arm that formed a "J." But the moles were natural.

"We also found these on both victims." He rolled the

36

body onto the left side, a black spider tattoo on the base of his neck.

"Both have the same marking?" Dolan asked.

"The exact tattoo in the same exact spot."

~~~~~~~~~

After I dropped Casey off I headed back to my place. While I sat at a light on Century Boulevard and La Brea, a woman crossed the street in front of my car holding the hand of a little girl wearing a pink dress. The ribbons in her pigtails bounced along with her hair. Claire always liked to put Ellen's hair in pigtails and dressed her in pink and white. I missed her little arms around my neck when I came home from the precinct. Every night she greeted me with, "Daddy! You need a shave." She would have been five next month. Right now Claire would be in the throes of planning a birthday party for her.

~~~~~~~~~

Dolan and I drove to the Sunset Tower Hotel to interview James Withers, the Carrington's accountant and attorney. I hope he'll have useful information on Otis. I wondered if it was a wise decision to entrust both the family's legal matters and finances to one person. The stop and go traffic heading west on Sunset was murderous at seven in the evening, but this guy wanted to meet us for cocktails and canapés. Dolan read it as a feeble attempt to intimidate us.

We parked four blocks away and congratulated each other for not having to trudge up and down the "Mighty" hills, but until I got my first advance from Marion, there was no way could we afford valet parking.

37

Once inside, the air conditioning and plush carpeting told me this place was definitely out of my league. We stopped and looked around at the framed paintings and tall, lush flower arrangements decorating the lobby.

Dolan said, "Hope he's paying for this little get together."

I told the desk clerk we were there to meet with Mr. Withers. He directed us to the dining room. Casey stood with his hands at his sides and looked around at the floor to ceiling windows with a view of Los Angeles. His eyes wandered to the tables covered in crisp white linen and filled with fine china and crystal glasses. "I feel like I did when I'd visit my grannie's." He put his hands behind him. "I might break something."

The Maitre'd approached, "You are waiting for Mr. Withers?" His eyes gave both of us a once over. Neither of us had on a tie or dinner jacket. But we were in pressed white shirts and sports coats.

"I'll show you to your table, Mr. Withers has been delayed." He didn't sound so much apologetic as reporting a fact, "This way please," and extended his arm.

Although he handed each of us a leather bound menu, we hesitated looking inside. The table was in the darkest corner, far from the windows. "I guess he didn't tip the Maitre'd," Dolan joked.

"You think maybe it's the way we're dressed?" I asked

Dolan's mouth fell open, "Is that Marlon Brando?" he whispered and pointed past me.

I brushed his arm down, "Stop pointing Casey. You've been around movie stars before, right?"

I turned around and noticed Eddie Fisher and Debbie

38

Reynolds, walking hand in hand. Eddie gave me a slight wave that was more a polite gesture than one of friendship.

"Eddie Fisher waved to you Sky." Dolan was acting like a silly high school girl, "Did you ever work with them? Bev loves his music. Could you get an autograph?"

"No. We're not friends, we only worked together."

Marlon was leaving and stopped beside our table to let the couple pass. He looked down and put his hand on my shoulder, "Hey, didn't we do a picture together?" I stood and shook his hand,

"That was several years ago Mr. Brando. It was only for a couple of days. I'm surprised you remembered." He headed for the lobby, but stopped and turned, "You stunt guys put your lives on the line for us actors. Sure I'd remember you," and left out the front door.

"Why didn't you introduce me, Sky?"

"Why? He doesn't know me. Did you hear him say my name?"

Casey looked over at Eddie Fisher, "What about them?" He pointed again.

"They're sitting at a table facing the window with their backs to the public. They don't want to be disturbed. Stop it."

He kept staring at them.

"Here," I stood and switched seats with Casey, "This way you don't have to look at them."

We heard the music from the bar, the wall was thin where we sat.

Another man stopped at our table, but I didn't recognize him.

"Gentleman, I'm James Withers." He was decked out in a dinner jacket, tie and all the accessories you could think of, including a fresh white rose in his lapel. With the thick, black framed glasses he wore and his light red hair and beard, he looked more like a raccoon. The way he stood behind his chair it seemed like he expected applause or something. Dolan picked up on it too. Being former cops, neither one of us stood, but since he was the money guy for the Carringtons, I half stood and shook his hand. He lit a cigarette, took one puff and coughed before he put it in an ashtray.

"I've taken the liberty of pre-ordering some canapés." Withers signaled the waiter and two plates of little sandwiches and deviled eggs appeared at the table.

"What are you gentlemen drinking?" He asked while holding a finger up to the waiter.

"Scotch." I replied. Casey said, "Not Scotch. Have you got any good Irish whiskey?"

The waiter replied, "Bushmill's and Jamesons sir, which do you prefer?"

"Jamesons, of course... and no ice."

"How much time do you have before your next engagement?" I asked.

Withers tugged his monogrammed sleeve, exposing a large gold cufflink and looked at his watch, a very expensive watch. "I can give you about an hour and a half at the most."

I downed a little sandwich and said, "I wanted to talk to you about Otis Carrington. Marion Carrington referred us to you regarding his disappearance." I slid a business card across the table. He read it and put it down.

40

"Yes, she called me, but I fear she's barking up the wrong tree. Chewy has a mind of his own. He's a very stubborn young man." He paused, "Don't get me wrong, he's a nice boy, amiable and appreciative of all Marion has done for him. But he can be too stubborn and independent for his own good."

Withers had a nice voice, maybe a radio trained voice.

"So, what else can you tell us?"

"He had no real friends in school, boys or girls. Chewy didn't participate in extracurricular activities or sports. He was a very private kid."

I looked closely at Withers. It was dark in the corner, but I did notice small close set eyes behind those glasses.

I could see he wasn't going to give us much, "Thank you, Mr. Withers for meeting with us and for..." I waved my hand over the food. "May I ask what your relationship is with the Carrington family?"

"I am their attorney, accountant and a long time friend of the family. I was close to Marion's late brother. I look after her fortune and...her, so to speak."

"We've met her two nieces at the house, they seem to do a good job caring for her."

"Loretta tries but isn't able to stand up to Marion. And Cassandra, well... she's just a waste of time. I think she hangs around waiting for Marion to die so she can get her inheritance."

"Inheritance? Do you think Cassandra could have something to do with Chewy's disappearance?"

He took a long moment to think. His voice cracked when he said, "Cassandra's obnoxious behavior is her way

41

of dealing with life. As sarcastic and arrogant as she is...she loves Chewy."

He paused, "Marion has been the legal guardian to Cassandra, Loretta and Otis. She inherited her three brother's children along with the family fortunes. My father promised her father he'd look after Marion if she remained unmarried. I took over that duty when my father died. I know it makes Marion look like a money hungry spinster. But remember, instead of enjoying the free lifestyle of a young woman with money to burn, she spent her time caring and nurturing those young people. She's a devoted aunt."

Dolan took a few notes on the back of a flyer he confiscated from the lobby.

Wither's looked at his watch, "Well Gentlemen, anything else I can answer for you?"

"Not at this time. Will you be available, if we have further questions?"

"Sure, anything for Marion. Just call for an appointment."

Chapter Five

Ciro's was just down the street. As we drove past, Casey said, "It's early, how about one more drink? On me." I hung a U-turn and parked. We walked a couple blocks and saw the double squared building with its flat roof.

The bar was in the back so we meandered through the dining room. In the corner of my eye, I noticed Marilyn Monroe sitting at a table laughing it up with some friends. Good thing Dolan didn't see her. Who knows what he would've done. We slid onto a couple stools and grabbed a handful of peanuts while the bartender poured our drafts.

I juggled a few peanuts in my hand, "What did you think of Withers?"

"His voice was familiar. Do you think he works in radio?"

"He's a lawyer, so he's probably trained his voice to, you know, do stuff in front of the jury." My mind went blank and my tongue felt like it was covered with fur. It could've been left over from the Scotch. "What do you think about the case and all?"

"You should take it. We need the money."

"Yeah, but Hawaii? It's so far."

Dolan made a face when he drank his beer. "I don't think I'll ever get used to this swill. Wish I could find a place that had Guinness on draft... and not refrigerated, mind you." He took another swallow and grimaced, "You said you had letters from the missing lad?"

I hadn't looked through them, and I really didn't want

to if I wasn't going to take the case. "I think it would be a waste of time." I stared at my beer. "Y'know... Dear auntie, please send money and all that."

"Sky, you should read them, see what's going on in the kid's life then make a decision," Dolan was always the voice of reason.

The show had started in the main room and the band leader cracked a few jokes before we heard him say, "We have a surprise visitor who's welcome any time. Give a warm welcome to Sammy Davis, Jr."

Dolan shot to his feet and stood by the doorway applauding with everyone else as the singer came out. We listened to him sing *Funny Valentine* from his latest album. My last evening out with Claire was on Valentine's Day, three days before the fire. I didn't feel so much like clapping and took another swallow of my beer.

~~~~~~~~~

The air conditioning was still out in our office building the next day, so I met Dolan for lunch at Al's Diner. We read through the twenty or so letters from Chewy Carrington to his Aunt Marion. Nothing indicated he was in distress or angry. What we saw was a young guy who enjoyed the beach, and made friends.

Dolan noticed that Chewy began all his letters with *Dear Family*, and closed with *Aloha*. "I always thought *Aloha* meant hello. Why would he close them with that word?"

"Oh yeah? I thought it meant Good bye. Guess I'll find out...if I go."

Casey didn't say anything. He just looked at me - waiting for something.

44

I took a deep breath and shoved the stack of letters to the center of the table. "All this. I just don't know. Maybe I won't take the case."

"Why?" Dolan picked up the letter, "You... we need the money Sky."

"Hell, I'd have to go to Hawaii. Last time I was there, Uncle Sam was shipping me off to Korea." I took a gulp of coffee, "Something's wrong...this whole setup smells. And you know I hate pineapple."

Dolan let out a belly laugh, "You need to take this case, chum. Besides, I'm stuck with that spoiled brat three more months. Go ahead. Take it. The Carringtons sound like they're up to their necks in dough. You go make some money, I'll take care of the business here and keep you informed if anything happens with your lawsuits." He leaned back, "You haven't taken any time off since Claire..." He paused, "You need to get away. Besides, I understand the Hawaiian language doesn't have the letter "y". So you'll be safe if you should happen to meet a Hawaiian girl." He laughed again.

Casey knew me all too well. I don't date ladies whose name end in "y". They've been bad luck.

"Man, you need a holiday - and a girl. Now - Go!"

~~~~~~~~

Before I left the office that evening, I made a list of reasons I shouldn't go. They were outnumbered by the one reason I should go, money.

I drove home along the coast. Hawaii was to my right across the ocean. I remembered it had great sunsets.

45

Chapter Six

I called Loretta Carrington and asked her to meet me at the same deli, this time for dinner.

"Would you bring Cassandra with you?"

She hesitated, "Sandy? I'd prefer not to at this point. Let's keep it to just the two of us."

It was after dark when I strapped on my shoulder holster, checked to be sure my gun was loaded and slipped into a sports jacket. I parked a block down Sunset from Greenblatt's and got that uneasy feeling I was being followed - but why? The deli was crowded and I was late. Loretta was waiting patiently. I slid into the booth. It was my turn to apologize. She acknowledged me with kind eyes and a smile. She'd done her hair up and looked like a movie star in her strapless yellow sundress. The fact that Loretta's name didn't end in "y" was a good thing. I didn't need more trouble. Before we ordered, I told her I'd decided to take the case.

"That's wonderful!" She reached across and put her hand over mine.

"So Loretta, how is this Hawaii trip going to work?"

"Please call me Lory, everyone else does."

Hold on, is that a "y" in her name? Maybe it ends in "I".

"If you don't mind, I'll stick with Miss Carrington for now." I was quiet for a long while. Lory was patient. "I'm going to need airfare and a place to stay. Does your family know anyone in the Honolulu Police Department? We can get this taken care of a lot faster if I have help from the

46

local authorities, and hopefully I won't have to be away long."

"I can arrange for your transportation and accommodations. You don't mind a hotel, do you?" She took a small pad from her purse. "Could you meet with me and Auntie one more time?"

I nodded. She wrote down a day and time and signed it, Lory Carrington. Wouldn't you know it - she used a "y".

It was after sunset but the street lights hadn't come on yet when I walked her out to her new Chevy hardtop. I watched her drive away before I headed back up Sunset to where I'd parked. As I searched my pocket for my key I heard footsteps closing quickly behind me. I turned and reached for my gun... too late. A hand grabbed my arm and pulled it behind me. Another covered my nose and mouth with the stunning smell of Ether, everything went dark.

When I came to, I felt myself being dragged along a road. My gun and one of my shoes was missing. My head throbbed, but I could make out a couple of guys as they lifted me by my legs. I squinted my eyes open and in the darkness, I was being dangled over the side of a cliff.

I was still seeing double, but able to mumble, "So, you gonna drop me off a cliff or what?" They stopped in mid motion, "Before you do, mind telling me why?"

"Drop your stinking lawsuit against the studio and we might reconsider."

Morehead warned me about something like this. My eyesight cleared up and I could make out two thugs with hats. Another hatter joined them. I decided to say nothing while I thought of a comeback. They each took a part of me, held me horizontal and dropped me on the grass.

"Do it or you die."

With that, they kicked me like they were rolling a log.

"Hey!" It was then I realized it was a steep hill. I hit the rocks and dry brush as I rolled. Folding my arms across my chest, I tried to cover my face and slow the speed of the roll. It worked. After what seemed like an eternity of tumbling and pummeling with stones, I finally came to a stop on concrete. Was I in the middle of a road? I uncovered my eyes and saw I was on the sidewalk of a deserted street. I spit out dried dirt and grit. The good news was that I was all in one piece. I laid there catching my breath and took inventory of my body. Nothing seemed broken, but I hurt like hell. I sat up on my knees with my legs under me. The world was still spinning. I saw a car approaching, struggled to my feet and waved it down. It pulled up in front of me and stopped. At least I'd get a ride back to town, I thought, until the same three guys in hats got out and picked me up off the ground.

"Are you kidding?" Without a word they opened the trunk, threw me in and slammed the lid shut. When they took off, I got bounced around inside and gagged on the smell of gasoline and exhaust. If I didn't die from the roll down the cliff, I was probably going to get asphyxiated from the fumes. After a time, the car stopped. I heard the doors open and close - footsteps, and the trunk lid opened. They yanked me out stood me up against my car on Sunset where I left it. One of the guys grabbed me by my shirt and growled, "Drop the studio lawsuit now or the next ride will be your last. Now get out of here."

They opened my car door, shoved me in, threw my

gun and keys at me. I yelled, "Hey! Where's my other shoe?" but they drove away. I picked the gun up but they'd removed the magazine. When I sat up my body ached. The fumes from the gasoline made my stomach churn. My head felt like it was coming apart. I wanted to punch their lights out but there were three of them. In my current condition, I wouldn't have bet on me as a winner.

My place was just a few blocks away. I made it home, dragged myself out of the car and limped to the door. There was a sheet of paper folded and tacked to it. I pulled it off and went inside.

After I pulled a cube steak out of the refrigerator, I flopped on the bed and gingerly placed the cold piece of meat over my face. Why would they go after some small fry like me. My lawsuit must've rattled some important cages. I planned to call my lawyer and let him know what happened. It would be the safe thing to do. Who knows what would happen next? I had no significant others left for them to go after, so why should I back down?

When my head stopped throbbing, I took the steak off my face and read the paper that was tacked on my door,

Sky, Meet me at the coroner's office tomorrow at 2:00 pm. Casey.

I reloaded my gun with a spare magazine and looked in my bathroom mirror. It was not pretty. I looked as though I'd lost a fight to a cement mixer. I downed some aspirin and passed out.

Chapter Seven

The next morning I looked in the mirror. It was scary. My face was swollen, scabby and bruised. I cleaned up as best I could.

A quick look out the window told me that Mother Nature was still at it. It's not supposed to rain in September. That's why I live in California. The radio was tuned to KFWB. I hoped to get a traffic report but got Fats Domino's *Ain't That a Shame* instead. My windshield wipers kept time to the song... this was going to be a very strange day.

I pulled into the Carrington's driveway, parked and took one last look at my face in the rear view mirror... disgusting. If this mug doesn't send the Carrington women running, then they've got more guts than I thought.

I navigated my way up to the door like the first time I was here. This time it was answered by a short, wiry man wearing a dark blue suit, white shirt and bow tie, "Mr. Drake?" He stared at me but said nothing about my face. Since he never saw me before, he probably thought I always looked like this and was being polite.

I stepped inside, shucked off my soaking wet rain coat and handed it to him. "And your name?

"Jonathan, sir. Please come this way." He led me to the same yellow and white striped room as before. "Please wait here." I looked around and stared out the window at the rain. I could get used to a place like this on a cold winter day with the fireplace crackling away. I heard the door open, I saw Cassandra. She slid into the room and closed the doors behind her. This time she wore a white kimono robe with a pink sash to tie it shut... only it wasn't, and what showed made it obvious that all she had on under it was a flimsy babydoll nightie. Sandy leaned back against the doors, a cigarette in one hand and a half full bottle of Burgermeister in the other.

"Hello Drake..." she took a long drag on her cigarette. "I gave Aunt Marion your message," She looked up at my face and took a couple of steps toward me. "Oh, poor Drake, what happened to your lovely face?"

I shrugged, "What message?"

She took a couple more steps and stopped to stub out her cigarette in an ashtray.

"I didn't leave a message."

"Sure you did." She downed the rest of her beer, slithered up close and whispered, "The one about you being thirty minutes late for your appointment." She put one hand on my shoulder while she slipped the other into the waistband of my pants. I grabbed it before it got too far down. She let her robe fall to the floor, "There's a lot we can do in thirty minutes." As she pressed her firm body against mine, she made another move for my waistband. This time I grabbed both her wrists and squeezed them tightly.

"You're drunk Miss Carrington. Stop acting like a cheap B-girl." She tried to knee me in the groin. I shoved her onto the settee. In a drunken attempt to sit up, she tumbled onto the floor, giggling. When I extended my hand to help her up, she fell back and laughed.

I left her in the center of the room and made an exit to the foyer where I waited for her Aunt.

Loretta appeared, as pretty as ever. This time Withers wheeled Marion into the foyer. Behind me, Cassandra was smoking, leaning on the door frame, as obnoxious as ever. She'd put her robe back on and this time tied it with a bow. Withers was dressed in a pin striped suit, white shirt with a fresh purple carnation in his lapel and a matching purple tie.

"Oh my, when did that happen to you Mr. Drake?" Loretta asked.

"Last night. Just a little accident."

"You've met Mr. Withers." Marion said. "James, I'm flying Mr. Drake to Hawaii to find Chewy. What have you found out thus far, Mr. Drake? You will assist us to locate Chewy?" Her question was more of a demand.

"Before I fly off to Hawaii in search of Otis, you should know I was at the Coroner's office and viewed the bodies of two young men whose descriptions were very close to Chewy's... I mean, Otis's." I showed Marion a photograph of one. "That is not Chewy." Marion said. James and the two nieces looked over Marion's shoulder. They let out a sigh and shook their heads. Marion closed her eyes and made the sign of the cross, "Thank God."

"I have one more photo. Remember, there were two bodies."

Marion opened her eyes and sat up straight. "All right, I'm ready."

I presented the second one. They stared at the photo. Cassandra gasped and ran out of the room, Loretta put her hand over her mouth and wept. Withers lit a cigarette and rested his hand on Marion's shoulder while she stared silently at the image.

"Both had matching tattoos and a series of small moles on their arms that formed the letter 'J'."

"This one looks very much like my Otis." Marion looked at me, "How did this man die?"

"He was shot in the back during a parade in San Pedro. The two were killed in the same manner, but in different locations. Do any of you know the identity of the other man?"

Withers, Marion and Loretta shook their head.

Withers coughed, put his cigarette down and asked. "Where does the trail lead?"

"I don't know yet."

Marion said nothing. She took a couple of deep breaths and crushed the photo in her fist, "If this is my Chewy, I want you to find the person who murdered him."

"Before we go off looking for a killer, someone from the family must go down to the Coroner's office and positively identify the body."

Marion sobbed into her handkerchief, "Take Sandy and Lory. I can't do that."

Withers knelt beside her and put his hand on hers, "Maybe you should give yourself some time, Marion. Don't rush into an investigation of this nature for a few days. Let them see if it's really Chewy before we do anything else."

Marion pulled her hand away and looked at me with fire in her eyes, "Young man, you are to do whatever it takes. I don't care about the cost."

"I appreciate your confidence in my abilities. We must, however, establish whether or not the body at the morgue is, in fact, your nephew. That's our first order of business." I called Logue and told him we were on our way to make an identification. Loretta was more than willing to drive, I suspect Cassandra didn't object because that left her hands free for other things, maybe?

Lory put the top down on her aunt's new Packard convertible after we all piled into the front seat. I didn't mind being driven downtown, sandwiched between two beautiful women. Before Loretta turned the ignition key, she looked at her cousin, "Sandy, keep your hands to yourself and act your age."

~~~~~~~~~

We parked, but before we went inside, I asked, "Have either of you seen a dead body before?" They shook their heads. Sandy mumbled, "I don't know if I can do this. I feel sick to my stomach."

I assured them the bodies had been cleaned and that all I needed was for them to tell us whether one of them was Otis or not. "Okay then. Let's get this over with." Lory opened her door and got out, but Sandy had her head down between her knees. Lory went around and opened the other door. With her hands on her hips, she said, "Well Sandy? Are you coming or not?" Sandy took a deep breath and sat up, pushing her hair back. I put my hand on her shoulder, "The sooner we do this, the quicker it'll be over."

Logue was standing with the door open in his long lab coat holding a clipboard. Sandy stopped. "I can't do this. I know I'll be sick." Dr. Logue saw this and handed each of

54

the women a mint candy. "Here ya go. This may help."

They each popped a mint in their mouth as I led them inside. The two bodies were on separate tables covered with white sheets stenciled with L.A. County Coroner. "Are we ready?" Logue asked, "I assume Sky told you what to expect." They nodded, even though Sandy had her eyes closed.

The doctor folded back the sheet enough to uncover the man's face and shoulders. I looked at the two women. Lory looked at his face, tilted her head and nodded before turning away. Sandy had a paper bag ready and opened her eyes. She let her hands drop to her side and stared at Otis. She too tilted her head and took a step closer. A tear drifted down her cheek. "May I touch him?" she asked Logue. He nodded. Sandy dropped the bag and tugged the sheet a little further to see the tattoo and moles on his arm. "Oh, Chewy - Who did this to you?" She straightened up and looked at me. "It's him," and walked out of the room with Lory.

"Well, that's that," Logue said and left with the cousins.

Lory put the top up for the drive back to the house. Neither one said a word but their faces were wet. I stayed silent and remembered when I had to identify the burnt bodies of my dear wife and sweet little daughter on those cold steel tables.

The two women ran into the house, leaving the front door wide open. I followed some distance back and found Lory hugging her aunt and sobbing. Marion looked up at me. Her tearful eyes were red with rage. I gave her a moment, "Do you still want me to go to Hawaii?"

"Yes, if that's what it takes! I want you to find the son-of-a-bitch who did this."

Sandy returned with a packed suitcase. "I'm going with you Drake."

"Hold on." I stood, "First, I work alone and secondly, anyone as emotionally involved in this case as you will get in my way."

Marion, as horrified as she was of Chewy's death, was more horrified Sandy wanted to go along. "Absolutely not Sandy, you'll just be a distraction and disrupt Mr. Drake's investigation. This is man's work." She insisted, "You'll stay here where I can protect you and Lory."

"Marion, please give this a few days." Withers insisted. "Don't make a hasty decision that you'll regret. I don't want you disappointed."

"My decision stays. How soon can you leave for the islands, Mr. Drake? Today? Tomorrow?"

"How much is this going to cost?" Withers asked.

I gave Marion a ballpark figure for two weeks over there. She waved it off, "The money doesn't matter, just do as I've asked."

Withers protested, but Marion yelled, "I've made my decision."

Lory showed me to the door.

Sandy was outside, leaning on my car, waiting with her suitcase.

"I'm going with you."

"Oh, no you're not. You heard your Aunt. It's too dangerous."

"I can take care of myself, Drake."

"How's your Judo, Karate? Know how to use a gun?" I pulled my coat aside to reveal my shoulder holster. "I don't think so," I added. "Especially not after your little display back in the morgue."

She was quiet. "If you don't take me with you, I'll persuade my aunt to hire someone else."

"Be my guest. I have plenty of other work I could take care of right here in L.A. So, go ahead - persuade. I don't mind at all, Miss."

"Your aunt is right Sandy, it's too dangerous," a voice came from behind. It was Withers with a cigarette in his hand. He stared at her until she picked up her suitcase and went back in the house.

In the daylight he looked different.

"Look, Drake. I care very much about Marion, I don't want to see her hurt or disappointed. She doesn't need to lose more sleep over this. As you can tell, her years are numbered," he paused, "I have a friend in the Honolulu Police Department."

"You should take care of that face," he said as I opened my door.

Chapter Eight

I drove back to the Coroner's office. Casey was waiting. Doctor Logue was washing his hands.

Nelson strolled in, "Good afternoon, Gentlemen."

Everyone looked at me. "What the hell happened to you?" Casey asked.

"I had a disagreement with some thugs last night. I'm okay." They kept staring at me. I pointed at the storage refrigerator, "I didn't want to say anything while the Carrington girls were here, but any luck identifying the weapon used on Otis Carrington and John Doe?"

"Actually," Logue said, "I was able to find out what the weapon was that killed them." He showed us a long metal tube with some kind of a mechanism at one end. "It's commonly called a Bang Stick. You said no shell casings were found at the scene, right? The lab didn't find rifling marks on the bullets I pulled out of the victims. These things are used by fisherman and divers to deter or kill sharks." He unscrewed the part of one end and took out a spent .45 caliber shell casing and put it back together. "This apparatus is called a powerhead and when you screw it onto a long pole like this, it's called a bang stick. It's used like a spear." He held it like he was holding a javelin, "You jab it at the fish like this," and jabbed it at the floor. *"Bang!* The bullet kills the fish. From the marks left around the wounds, I'm pretty sure one of these killed them."

Dolan held the stick, "Do they do underwater spear fishing in San Pedro, Doc?"

"No. Out on Catalina Island maybe, but not so much here."

"If powerheads aren't used in San Pedro, then why..."

"So what's going on in San Pedro that the police aren't looking at Catalina," I asked.

Nelson jumped in, "There aren't any big fish that close to Catalina Island, except for whales but fisherman don't bother with them. These things are used to kill sharks that harass the fishermen and their catch. They aren't used for small fish because they'll just blow up. Some bang sticks use shotgun shells, but these poor souls," he took the stick and pointed it at the bodies, "were killed with a .45. Besides, most of the fishing fleets have been grounded for a few days because of the century rain and storm off shore."

"Personally, I think both these victims are Hawaiians." He took an envelope from a table and emptied the contents into his hand, "They both wore one of these around their neck." In his palm he held a woven cord, attached to it was a tiny colorful shell.

"What is that, a seashell?" I asked. "Kinda little."

The doctor held it up to the light, "I did some research and made a few calls. It's a Decatopecten Noduliferum, more commonly called a Sunrise shell and comes from a specific type of small scallop native only to the deep waters around Hawaii."

"What? That tiny thing?" Casey asked. "It's just a seashell. You can find them anywhere. There are millions of them on the beaches around here."

"Not like these." Doctor Logue said as he slid it from his palm back into the envelope. "Typically, they're found at sunrise - hence their name; and the colors of the shells also look very much like a sunrise. They're extremely rare and were considered to be sacred by the ancient Hawaiian People. So these men either just got back from or were on their way back to the Hawaiian Islands. Not sure which, but then - that's your job, right?"

I showed him a picture of Chewy at eighteen years old. Doc held it by Otis, "Yep, this one could very well be the Carrington boy." He pointed with his pinky, "See the nose and bridge?"

"Then, who's the other poor unfortunate soul?" Dolan asked.

Doc shrugged, "I have no idea."

~~~~~~~~~

If Casey was going to take care of things while I was in Hawaii, I had to get my files and paperwork straight. I called both my lawyers and instructed them to stay in contact with Casey while I was away.

Since my exercise gym was vandalized last month, I've been waiting for the insurance company to pay for repairs. Until then, I'm closed.

Back at my place I made tea and sat on the sofa thinking of Hawaii. I was a young Marine fresh out of boot camp, relaxing in Waikiki. I had no clue of what awaited me in Korea. My chest tightened as I watched the steam circle from my cup. The memories of rotten wood and mold invaded my head. As I look back, Hawaii was the jumping off point to hell.

~~~~~~~~~

It was noon when Casey parked at the Los Angeles International Airport. "By the way," he handed me a small

60

envelope, "James Wither's called with the name and telephone number of his contact at the Honolulu PD. The name is Sanoe Fan."

"I'll call him when I get there."

I got out of the car, grabbed my overnight bag and told Casey about my encounter with the two studio goons.

"Why didn't you tell me about this before now?" He took a deep breath, "Then it's good that you leave town. Let things cool down."

I didn't want any surprise visits to Casey since he had nothing to do with either case. I gave him a pat on the back. "You sure?"

"Don't worry Sky, I can handle any problem that comes up."

"Be careful, they may come looking for me and find you. Be sure to keep me posted - daily if need be."

He took my arm and dragged me into the terminal, "Just telegraph your contact info, and don't worry yourself over the lawsuits. Remember, both your lawyers said it will take a while." We checked in at Will Call where Marion had my ticket waiting.

We walked toward the plane, "Take a few days to yourself and try to find a girl. It should be easy with few of them whose names end in 'y'." I punched him the arm. He frowned at me, "I'm serious Sky."

We stopped at the bottom of the gangway, Casey motioned me to get on the plane. After a deep breath, I climbed the steps of the huge four-engine, Pan American Clipper. At the top, I stopped and waved to Casey. He gave me a quick salute and went inside. That was that. I'd be in

Honolulu in a little more than six hours. It took days by ship.

A beautiful young stewardess named Lucy showed me to my seat...First Class!

She explained the seatbelt and fluffed a pillow for my head, "After we're in the air, I'll be serving champagne."

I found a copy of the *Honolulu Star-Bulletin* in the seat back pocket. There was an article about the investigation into a MATS plane crash back in March. I already hated to fly and I didn't need to read about planes crashing in Hawaii. The Marines must've thought I was too valuable to take that chance and sent me to Korea on a ship.

The man in the seat next to me was busy reading the Wall Street Journal. I chose to not disturb him, besides, what would we talk about?

I heard the big engines start up. The whole airplane shook to life. I signaled the stewardess.

"Have you got anything stronger, like Scotch?"

"Of course... as soon as we're airborne."

"...and make it a double."

After a few safety announcements by the captain, we began to move. We rumbled down the concrete until I felt the airplane lift off the ground. I closed my eyes as the roar of the engines settled into a distant drone.

I felt a soft hand on my shoulder. "Would you like that drink now?" I thought I was dreaming. She returned immediately with my scotch. I downed it and sat back.

"Excuse me Mr. Drake, would you care for lunch?" I blinked my eyes open and looked at my watch it was 2 pm. Our lunch was served on China dishes and silverware.

Lasagna, salad and coffee, and cookies. I tried not to seem overly impressed to the people around me. They appeared to be used to this sort of thing. As we ate, the man by the window turned and introduced himself. He owned some shoe company and just started selling rubber sandals in Hawaii. I guess he could tell I wasn't excited about the shoe business and went back to his reading. Across the aisle was a younger guy. I introduced myself. He said his name was Johnny Burnette. I'd heard his music on the radio. I was surprised I didn't recognize him, though he looked unkempt. He told me he had a stopover in Honolulu, then he was off to entertain our boys stationed in Japan. When I asked about his band, he pointed a thumb behind him, "Oh, they're back in the regular seats. I'd be with them but my agent said it would look better if I sat up here in first class." He shrugged, "Go figure." I told him a little about my TV program and my movie stunt work. Now this guy and I had something in common, show business. We griped about our agents for a while. I looked at my plate and thought how Claire would have loved a trip like this. She always wanted to go to Hawaii. I lost my appetite and went downstairs to the lounge for another drink.

I met a couple on their way home to Honolulu from a trip to the new Disneyland. It sounded like something little Ellie would have liked. Why was I feeling like this? Was it guilt for having a good time? Maybe it was the Scotch. I was getting tired and we had another three hours before landing in Honolulu. I went back up to my seat. Lucy helped turn the sleeperette into a bed and even brought me a small blanket and pillow. She turned off the overhead light and I fell asleep thinking about what I'd been missing in life.

The stewardess patted me on the arm, "Sir it's time to wake, we will be landing in less than an hour." She handed me a warm towel moistened with a lemony fragrance. This was world's better that the train to Santa Rosa. I could get used to this.

~~~~~~~~~~

I was greeted by a warm, sea breeze as I staggered down the gangway stairs. The smell of flowers was in the air as I walked across the concrete apron. A pretty island girl escorted each of us into the First Class area of the terminal where waiting island girls placed a flower lei around my neck with a kiss on both cheeks. This is not the way I remembered Hawaii the last time I was through here, but then again, I was carrying my rifle and all my gear.

I perused the lobby until I found the exit to the street, and heard someone shout my name. I looked around. Who in this place knew my name?

Above the heads of people in front of me, I saw an arm holding a straw hat waving up and down.

"Mistah Drake! Mistah Drake!"

I parted the waiting crowd and followed the voice to a smallish women with almond shaped eyes, and skin as white as could be. She was holding a piece of cardboard with my name stenciled on both sides. "Mistah Skylah Drake?" she yelled. I walked up to her. She was probably not even five feet tall.

I looked down at the top of her head, "I'm Skylar Drake."

She jumped back, "Ah, Mistah Drake, I am Leilani," she held out her hand. No smile.

"You must be tired from your flight." Still no smile.

I looked up at the sun. "What time is it anyway?"

"It is still afternoon." The little China doll answered, "Only four o'clock local time."

Leilani took my bag with both hands. She was strong for a tiny woman, and walked to the door where she stopped. She turned around, looked back at me and motioned with her head, "Come on. I will take you to your hotel. You stay at the Waikiki Biltmore. First I drop you off. Laytah somebody pick you up for dinner."

She opened the back of a pre-war panel truck parked at the curb. It looked to be an old bakery van. The bottoms of the fenders and running boards were rusted away.

"Come on, get in. We gotta go. You want me to get a ticket?"

She hopped up onto a wooden soda pop crate she'd put on the driver's seat and pumped the accelerator a couple times with her toes. "Okay, here we go," and turned the key. The passenger side door creaked and groaned in protest when I pulled it open. The old truck coughed to life. She was so short she had to look through the steering wheel to see.

I looked out the windows at swaying coconut trees, tourists and more Asian faces than I'd seen since I was in Korea and Japan. She chattered on, but I could barely understand her. So, this is Paradise.

Soon she pulled up to what looked like a brand new hotel. A uniformed valet in white gloves came to my side, took a rag out of his pocket to open my door, while another went around and helped Leilani out of the truck, "Aloha Auntie," The valets greeted her like she was one of the owners. "You must be working today," one of them commented. She looked back at the truck, "My apologies for parking the junker out front. I was on North Shore this morning and you know how they get when fancy haole car shows up in their neighborhood.

"Come, follow me," the valet said. "We'll get you checked." I nodded and followed him to the desk. He exchanged some comments and nods with the smiling manager as he held a fountain pen at the ready. A porter took my bag, "You have a couple of hours to kill before dinner. You can take a swim, shop for souvenirs or have a nap. You will be picked up around six."

The porter opened the doors to an air-conditioned, ground floor room with sliding glass doors that opened onto the pool deck. I stopped, "Are you sure this is the right room?" He nodded and set my bag on a luggage stand. I flipped him a quarter tip. I'll have to write and thank Marion for the generous digs. I looked out the doors at the sparkling pool. Families and their kids were whooping it up and splashing water everywhere. I took off my tie and unpacked. I asked the Hawaiian shirted concierge where to get some shirts like his. He suggested I walk down Kalakaua Avenue. I thought it might be a good idea to blend in and got one of those silk Hawaiian shirts with pineapples and coconut trees on it for dinner tonight.

~~~~~~~~~

I got back to my room and took a nap. My phone woke me up at a quarter to six. It was the front desk clerk telling me that a Sanoe Fan was waiting. The name bounced off my brain as I slowly came to. After I splashed water on my face, I ran my hands through my hair and threw on my new Hawaiian shirt. When I asked for Sanoe Fan at the desk, a woman in a long floral dress approached with a flower lei in her hands.

"Aloha Mr. Drake, I'm Sanoe Fan."

Sanoe Fan was a woman? She put the lei over my head and kissed me on the cheek.

"I'm with the Akau Kaona Police Department." She was little with two sets of dimples each time she smiled. Her boy cut hair was brushed back on the sides

All I could get out was, "I'm pleased."

"So, you're a friend of James Withers?" She gave me an up and down look, "I see you adapted to the local color quickly. That's perfect for dinner tonight... I'm taking you to a Luau."

I'd seen Luaus in movies but never actually been to one. We walked down the beach a short distance to what looked like a big party. Everyone sat on mats at long tables overflowing with food, fruit and drinks. We ate and laughed until the hula show started. This was a great welcome, but I was anxious to get to work on the case. I looked around at the tourists packing in the food like there was no tomorrow and wondered what secrets all this touristy glitz covered up.

<u>Chapter Nine</u>

Tonight I'd let myself relax and get to know my chaperone a little better, which didn't take long. I sat cross legged next to Sanoe. She picked up the drink in front of her in a coconut shell decorated with flowers, and a little umbrella. "Here's to a great time in Hawaii!" I picked up the one in front of me and toasted her. "Have you been to Hawaii before, Detective?"

The sugary cocktail made me wince. That much fruit juice and rum was harder to swallow than straight Bourbon, "I came through here with the Marines a few years ago on my way to Korea," I choked. "But it wasn't as nice as this. By the way," I held up my coconut, "What is this?"

"That's a Mai Tai."

"Whew," I coughed, "that's not like any Mai Tai I've had back in California!"

"Well, drink up, we go to work tomorrow." When I set my drink down and looked up, platters of food started to travel down the long table towards us. To be polite, I took a little. Sanoe explained each dish, including a thing called Huli Huli Chicken. "This is brand new and invented right here in Hawaii by good friends of mine. Once you taste it, you won't be able to stop." She was right, but there was one thing I couldn't bring myself to try... Poi. It had the consistency of library paste, but Sanoe told me it was considered the official food of Hawaii. If I didn't, at least try it, I would offend the Gods and everyone at the Luau. I took two fingers and scooped up a dab. I was right... library paste. It must be an acquired taste. They passed around something called Haupia, little white squares nestled in purple flowers that tasted like coconut gelatin.

Soon a beautiful island girl danced a graceful hula while tiki torches twirled in the background. Sanoe's big brown eyes sparkled from the light of the flames.

After the show we strolled back to my hotel. She reminded me before she left, "See you tomorrow for lunch with the Akau Kaona Captain of Police..."

"Lunch? Do you people do anything else here besides eat... and Aka what? Not Honolulu?"

"No, Akau Kaona is a separate town, own police force and Captain. We are so close to Honolulu and Waikiki that most people confuse us. Be ready at noon." She tugged at the sleeve of my new aloha shirt, "but, don't wear this, okay? You got a plain white shirt?"

It was midnight, I couldn't sleep and went to the bar for a beer. I sat by the radio and listened to music while I watched the moon on the water.

I rummaged through some pieces of today's newspaper sprawled along the bar, slated for the trash. Luckily I found the front page. It seemed the FBI was looking for a fugitive. Nancy Easton was on the lam since 1952 and was found to be in the Los Angeles area. If anyone recognized her or knew her whereabouts, they were asked to contact the nearest law enforcement agency.

I just about spilled my beer. It was a photo of me talking to that helpful nurse, at the accident the other day. I was floored when I focused the light on the portrait of the woman. It was her but not bleached blonde, they described her as a 5'4" redhead. Since I didn't know her whereabouts, I decided to do nothing, but the story had made it all the way to Hawaii!

I noticed a bunch of Japanese singing and whooping it up. I thought I was back in Tokyo on R&R.

I ordered another beer and went out to the quiet patio. It was dark. The full moon shined on the ocean and a path leading to the shore. I spotted a woman with hair down to her hips alone at a table. It was the only table not full of people. "Do you mind if I join you Miss?"

She smiled and gestured to the empty chair across the table.

I introduced myself just as simply, Sky. She smiled, "I'm Penny."

Unbelievable. Of all the women in Hawaii, I found one with a name that ended in "y".

Her eyes went straight to my hand and my wedding ring. "You're married," she said as if I had spinach stuck in my teeth.

I looked down at my ring. "I'm a widower." I didn't want to go into it.

"I'm sorry," she said in a more sympathetic tone.

"Thanks. Do you live here or just visiting?"

She smiled, "Depends what happens in the next few days. How about you?"

Penny had a Hawaiian accent and looked part Asian. I explained that I was a private investigator, here on a job for a client in L.A.

"You seem to be at a crossroad in your life. Do you have any idea what you want?"

70

She nodded and told me a story about her dream of owning a dance studio to teach Hawaiian dance and music. The territorial government was giving her a hard time over it, but all the people wanted it for their community.

I leaned forward, "You're a real lady, lovely, articulate, and you seem very smart. You can achieve anything you put your mind to. Go after your dreams. They can come true."

Her head snapped in my direction like she never heard that before. "Thank you, Sky, I appreciate your encouraging words."

She looked at her watch and stood, "I'm sorry, but I need to catch the next bus."

I set my bottle on the table, "I'll walk you to your bus."

She was quiet during the short walk, we waited in line. She continued her silence. As the bus pulled up, she held out her hand, I took it in both my hands. "Thank you again Sir." It was small and soft. Her eyes were filled with hope, "Remember," I said once more, "stick with your dreams."

Penny looked back and smiled as she stepped up into the bus.

As it drove away, I put my hands in my pockets and wondered why her name had to end in "y"? Was this some kind of sign?

After a nice cool shower in my room, I hit the sheets. As I drifted off, a thought came to me and I sat up, "What's wrong with my Hawaiian shirt?"

<u>Chapter Ten</u>

The ringing of the phone woke me up from a great dream of walking on the beach with Claire. Sun streaming between the slats of the shutters made me jump out of bed and grab my watch. With just enough time to meet Sanoe, I put on my clean white shirt and bought a cup of coffee at the bar to help me wake up. It didn't help. After all that, Sanoe was ten minutes late. I cooled my heels on the patio just off the lobby. With the soft tropical breeze and sun on my face, I was sorry she showed up at all. The weather was already getting too warm and uncomfortable for my shirt and tie. I really hated to leave, but there she was out of uniform.

The streets on the way to the police station, were lined with a jumble of one and two story buildings, and lots of trees, strange looking trees. Sanoe was talking about something, I nodded to be polite but had no idea what she was saying. I put my head back, *Come on Drake, snap out of it*. Could this feeling be due to the time difference?

She pointed to a strange looking mountain off to the east, "That's what we call Diamond Head."

"Are there really diamonds under there?" As the words fell out of my mouth, I realized how stupid it sounded. She looked at me, "Sky, you sure are gullible for a cop," as she pulled up to a single story brick building. I followed her inside through a swinging door. Captain Danny Liu was waiting, all smiles and enthusiasm. He reminded me of a dog greeting his master after a day's absence. He put his hand on my shoulder and introduced me around. He too, was not wearing a typical police issue uniform, but a low key aloha shirt with his ID clipped to his pocket. I pointed at my tie. "With the heat and humidity here, I guess it's a lot easier to work in casual clothes, am I right?"

"What casual?" he frowned, "I have my shirt tucked in."

Sanoe followed us to his office. He opened the window to a cool breeze and ocean view. "You can take off the tie if you wish, Detective." I was glad to hear those words. As fast as I could I untied it, stuffed it in my pocket and undid the top button of my shirt.

Sanoe began, "James Withers, our friend on the mainland, briefed me on what you have."

"How do you know Withers?" I asked.

"His father was a frequent visitor here."

Captain smiled, "He was friend of my father's and our family, JB, we called him. We were surprised when he passed. He was the picture of health. James was away at college most of the time. Didn't surprise me when his son took over the business."

Sanoe said, "We're prepared to assist in any way we can. I trust your accommodations are satisfactory?"

"Yes, very much so." I really wanted to get on with the investigation so I reviewed the photos of the two victims, the bang stick, and what I knew of the Carrington family. After several moments of dead air, I asked, "Do you have any questions for me?"

I filed away my papers and photos, I looked out the window thinking of places where I should start while I waited in silence for them to answer. They looked at each other, shrugged and... nothing. I felt like I was wasting Marion's time and money.

"Where would you suggest I begin the investigation?" I asked the Captain.

"I'll leave that up to you and Sanoe. This evening, you're invited to a dinner party. As far as the investigation, Lt. Peter Amano will take it from here. What do you think Sanoe?"

She nodded.

After the Chief treated us to lunch at a Chinese place, Sanoe deposited me at the precinct or station, or whatever they call it here, and introduced me to Lt. Amano,

"Call me Pete."

He was a wiry white guy with a big smile and definitely not Hawaiian. He was dressed like the other cops I've met so far. He lit a new cigarette while the stub of the old one still smoldered on his lips.

He shook my hand, "Always a pleasure to meet a man after my own heart. I'm a transplant from Pittsburgh. This place is as close to paradise as anyone can get. Sad you won't be here very long, Drake. You know, there's a lot to be said for Hawaii. It's not such a backwater as many people think. Just because we're farther from land than any other place on Earth..."

I was getting more anxious the more he talked. I didn't want to appear rude , but he went on and on. I glanced at my watch, "Would you look at that, it's two p.m. already. I really want to plan the investigation."

"Sure," Pete crushed out the stub with his fingers, "I'll

take you to the place where Carrington was last seen alive. I didn't know Chewy well, just met him a few times. He seemed like a nice guy, but sometimes he seemed a bit off, like he was thinking of something else when I talked to him." He held up a brown stained finger.

"Could you wait here a moment? I have some paperwork to sign off on. Shouldn't take too long," and reached over the counter, "Here, occupy yourself with the newspaper and I'll be right back." He left in a cloud of smoke.

I sat back and read about the former Mayor's speech promoting statehood for Hawaii. In another article, the boys in Washington D.C. rejected the idea of Hawaii and Alaska becoming States. I was guessing not many of those old hacks in D.C. have ever been here. All they know is the newsreels of Pearl Harbor being bombed. They'd change their minds in a flash if they knew what a Paradise this was.

Two hours later... Pete came bouncing up, "Ready to go?" He was smokeless!

That was a long few minutes but I said nothing. I've already learned to adjust my thinking to island time and their clocks moved slowly.

Outside, we stopped at a Chevy station wagon. POLICE was painted on the door. I stood back, "Is this for your surfboards?"

"Ha ha," he answered and lit another cigarette, blowing a perfect smoke ring. "We get that from all the kids. Seriously, this was all the dealer had and it does the job of two vehicles." The drive only took eight minutes but with Pete going on about everything from breweries to tourist spots, it seemed like forever.

It was after four when we pulled up and parked in front of a sleazy bar in a rundown part of town. We stepped over a couple bums drinking the last drops from bottles they probably dug out of the trash. The perfume of fresh flowers now reeked of stale B.O. and urine.

Pete put his sunglasses in his pocket, "This is Hotel Street. It's really several blocks." The sign above the door said, *ATLANTIS BAR, Home of the Best Mixologist in Honolulu.*

Mixologist?" I asked him as we slalomed around a couple more bums.

"Yea, we call bartenders mixologists here." We walked up to an grimy red door that hadn't seen a scrub brush in years. He paused with his hand on the handle, threw his spent cigarette on the sidewalk and looked at me. "Not much we can do now, but did anybody ever tell you that you look like a cop?" I didn't know if that was a compliment or a slam. "Hopefully you won't scare everybody in the place."

I guess it was a slam.

We entered a dark, smoked filled room with a definite sweet smell of something that wasn't tobacco. Music came from a juke box. As my eyes adjusted to the darkness, I could see a mirror ball sparkling onto the men and women crowded on the small dance floor. A couple of sailors were lined up at the bar, drinking and eating hard boiled eggs. I guess anything is better than C rations.

I did my best to follow Pete as we meandered to the bar, "Mitt," he yelled. A really big Hawaiian sauntered over to us wiping his hands on a towel. Three of me would probably fit in him. He must have been 6' 4" and his biceps were bigger than my thighs, maybe three hundred pounds.

"Hey," Pete said, "Dis haole guy coming from L.A. for do some work here." I barely understood what they said.

The guy looked up from under his heavy brow, "Hey, howzit?" and made a strange sign with his pinkie and thumb.

Pete turned to me, "He said hi." I waved a hand at him. "We interviewed this guy a few days ago. He's good."

The big man motioned us to the back room. The hall was even darker. I felt behind me to be sure my gun was nestled in my belt.

He switched on the light. A sickly sweet smoke filled the cramped room. The shelves were lined with canned Spam, several deep

"What you want to know?" Mitt stood, with his brawny arms folded over his chest.

I opened my mouth to speak when Pete interrupted. "Hey Bra, jes tell him same like you tell us."

Pete seemed to turn that pidgin English on and off. I remembered hearing something like that when I came through here with the Marines.

Mitt went on with words that made no sense.

"According to the big Hawaiian," Pete translated in my ear, "Chewy stopped in here for a drink with a friend the evening before he flew to L.A."

Mitt was chewing on something, Pete continued to translate, "They got in a fight with a bunch of sailors but Mitt chased all six of them out with a crowbar."

Both of them just stared at me. "That's it?" I muttered.

77

"What else you want to know, eh?" Mitt asked.

"How often was Chewy here?"

"He come here alone for drinks. Sometime bring a friend."

"Apparently Chewy was a mean drunk," Pete added, "and fought with everyone, every time."

"How often did he win?" I asked.

Mitt chuckled, "You don't know da guy do you?"

I shook my head.

Pete interrupted, "Carrington was known in these parts as a hell raiser and could take care of himself and anyone he chose."

My gut told me something was wrong with this situation and the discussion. Mitt was holding something back. So was Pete. I decided to let it go for now. Pete escorted me to the front room. Mitt poured us a whiskey on the house.

Everyone was smiles and pats on the back. My drink tasted off - maybe it was local whiskey. I followed Pete to a table when a good-looking brunette appeared in front of me. "Hey, sailor," she slid onto a chair beside me, "Don't mind if I do." She took my hand and finished my drink while I was still holding it. When an old tango came on the jukebox, she tossed the empty glass to the side and snuggled against me.

"That's better," she whispered and tugged my arm toward the dance floor.

"Sorry, I don't dance," and tried to peeled her off of me.

"Says who?"

Before I could protest again, we were in the middle of

the floor with her arms and legs twisted around me. I was stuck, literally bound by the woman. I looked around for Pete, he was entangled with another woman. The smell of cheap perfume was nauseating. As the music went on, she loosened her hold. Her hands went to her hair and fluffed it on top of her head. She pulled away and twirled by herself. With her hair up I noticed a black spider tattoo on the back of her neck. I looked for a way off the dance floor, but it was jammed shoulder to shoulder. She put her arms back around my neck, "So sailor, who was the jerk that said you couldn't dance?" and planted a wet one on my lips. I grabbed her arm and dragged her to the light.

"Hey!" she wrapped herself around me again. "What's the idea? Don't you want to have a little fun? It'll only cost you five dollars."

I turned her around, held her shoulder with one hand and lifted her greasy hair with the other. Just like Chewy and the other victim's tattoo, a black spider.

"So you like it rough, hey sailor?" and planted another kiss on my mouth.

"Where did you get that tattoo?"

She stomped on my foot with her spiked heel and yelled, "Go to hell," before she ran off.

The pain ran from my foot to my shins. I spotted Pete, who was enjoying the company of a redhead a bit too much. I grabbed him and took him outside.

"What the hell is this place?"

"Just a lounge." He looked up, laughed and lit a smoke.

"A lounge? Try a cat house."

I followed him to his car while I tried to wipe the sticky cheap lipstick off my mouth.

"So, what's the deal Pete? Is it a brothel or not?"

He didn't answer.

<u>Chapter Eleven</u>

I took his keys and cigarette from him, and put him in the back seat where he passed out. The guy was a lightweight. With him as useless as a canned sardine, I found my way back to my hotel and tried to come up with a plan to sober him up before the dinner party.

The valet saw who was in the back.

"It's Lt. Amano," I said, "he's drunk."

I slipped him the keys and a dollar bill, "Could you take him around back, out of sight and splash some water on him? When he wakes up, give him a lot of black coffee." I gave the boy another buck, "Call my room when he's awake."

He looked at the money in his palm, "Yes sir, Mistah Drake."

As soon as I got to my room I heard a big splash. I looked out my French doors, there was Pete writhing in the pool. Not quite what I meant but I guess it works.

After a cool shower, I changed into my Hawaiian shirt for the party. The phone rang. The valet called to tell me Pete was awake and very unhappy. I found him sitting behind the wheel of the police station wagon, sopping wet holding a cup of coffee.

"How did I get here and where the hell are my keys?" he mumbled.

The valet slipped me the keys. I held them up. "You ready to talk about the case and that Bordello?"

He shook his head, "It's no big deal, we talk about it

81

later. For now we eat, dance and sing. Enjoy life!" He reached into his wet pocket, "Got any smokes?"

The Captain's house was perched on the coast near Hawaii Kai, a big house for a captain's salary. I enjoyed the view while Pete slipped away. A few minutes later he appeared, dry and clean shaven. Pete acted like he lived here. I heard the screen door open and slam shut. The Captain strolled in wearing a flowery white Hawaiian shirt and white trousers.

He took a cold beer out of an ice bucket for himself, and two more for us. "Good, you're here." I wiped the bottle on my pant leg. After he cracked open his beer, he tossed us the bottle opener. Everyone seemed real cozy with one another. I thought that only happened in Hollywood and it wasn't real.

Three little girls came bouncing in, "Hi grandpa," and climbed on his lap giggling.

He set his beer on the counter and bent down to gather them up in his arms for a hug, "Ah, here's my pineapple, my guava, and my banana." He picked them up and twirled around.

My little Ellen use to climb up my leg, squirm on my lap, and stand on her little chubby legs to give me a hug. I could feel her little arms round my neck, and her curls tickling my cheek.

"You have little ones at home, Mr. Drake?" the Captain asked.

I shook my head.

A tiny woman in a flower print dress swished into the room, "Here is my wife, Leilani." He set his squealing grandchildren on the floor, and put his arm around her, "Leilani, this is Skylar Drake, from Los Angeles."

"Yah, I know. Remember? I pick you up at airport."

All cleaned up, I didn't recognize her. "Thank you for your help yesterday afternoon, Mrs. Liu."

The Captain looked around, "Where is niece?" he asked his wife. She answered in another language. He nodded to her and looked at me, "Everybody ready to go?"

I looked down at my Hawaiian shirt, "Is this going to be okay? My only suit is in my hotel room."

"You fit in just fine." Leilani patted me on the arm.

As buzzed as he was, Pete drove us to a large house near Kapiolani Park. I could hear music coming from inside. I followed them around back which I thought was a bit odd. A warm glow streamed from the open windows and the pathway was lit with tiki torches. The backyard...it stretched to the ocean! Waves lapped at the edge of the lawn. A string quartet played on the second story balcony. Long tables covered with food and flowers, like the one at the luau, stood in the center of the lawn. I could get used to this.

Captain introduced me to our host, Mayor of Akau Kaona, Rene Du Forrest and his wife, Helen. "His whole family is from the mainland," Pete slurred into my ear, "You know...Haoles."

More people arrived and I heard a lot of accents I hadn't heard before. Each time someone new arrived, I was introduced like I was some sort of a celebrity. Mayor Du Forrest and his wife made a point of explaining that I was here to investigate the death of Otis Carrington. The couple spoke perfect English but with an unusual accent. I was surprised that so many people seemed to know Chewy.

The guests turned their attention toward the house. I checked to see where they were looking when the mayor raised his glass, "Ah, my pride and joy," He embraced a lovely young woman who had entered wearing a flowing sarong. "My daughter, Vanessa."

She smiled and greeted each person with a handshake or nod. It was easy to see why he was proud of his beautiful daughter. She extended her hand, "You must be the Mr. Skylar Drake I've heard so much about. Welcome to Paradise."

I've only been here a day. Word travels fast.

The music stopped. Suddenly a chorus of male voices floated through the backyard. "Oh, The Gleeman of Hawaii, my favorite local group." Vanessa took my hand and turned toward the house. Come Mr. Drake, follow me." I looked back at Mrs. Du Forrest.

She smiled, "You young ones go ahead," and shooed us toward the music.

French doors surrounding the conservatory were open, the evening breeze flowed through as we sat listening to the group sing Hawaiian songs. Vanessa's long golden brown hair was loosely braided and drawn over one shoulder. I chose to look away every time she happened to glance my way.

"Come Mr. Drake. Let's dance." She pulled me to the dance floor. I wasn't sure how to dance to the Hawaiian music, but then, a different group sprung into a Cha-Cha. She made the small space between us seem even smaller.

"I'm not much of dancer," I choked.

"If you're that uncomfortable, come. I have something to show you." We walked along the shiny hardwood floors into a gallery. "I rather prefer being considered a painter and hope to attend the Cooper Union in New York some day."

Her work was pretty good, mostly landscapes of tropical islands. "That's quite a prestigious school, Miss Du Forrest." I knew Claire would have enjoyed discussing art with her.

"No need to be so formal, Mr. Drake. Please call me Vanessa."

"Well, Vanessa, my late wife was a painter," I took a breath, "Did you paint these views from the house?"

"Some yes, some no."

The music began again. She kicked off her high heels and took my hand. "No one can see you dance but me." We swayed around the room with the gentle sea breeze from the open French doors. Her hair brushed against my face. I closed my eyes suddenly transported to another place.

"Drake!" someone screamed from outside.

Vanessa pulled away from me. "You're needed," and pointed to a group of people pulling something out of the bushes.

She grabbed my hand and led me through the house to the backyard where I muscled my way through the crowd. The body of a young woman was on the ground clothed in a red cotton dress. She was pale and bluish. Her eyes were bulged, her tongue swollen, but she wasn't wet. I bent down to feel for a pulse in her neck...nothing. I could hear approaching sirens. I stood and said, "It's too late for help.

Looks like she may have been suffocated... Anyone know who she is?"

The Captain looked at me, "You mean to tell me you don't know?"

"Why should I know, I just got here yesterday."

He handed me two blood stained Polaroid pictures folded in quarters, "These were nailed to her forehead and chest."

I unfolded them, one was a photo of a China teacup and saucer on what looked like the table in my kitchen back in L.A. A pair of military dog tags were hanging over the rim of the cup. The second photo was a close up shot of the dog tags... my dog tags.

A woman's voice said, "That is Mai Le, girlfriend of Otis Carrington." She pushed through the crowd, "and my daughter."

I looked around for the Captain and Pete, but they'd disappeared. Sanoe pushed through the crowd and flashed her badge. In a cocktail dress and makeup, I didn't recognize her at first. My head was still pounding with anger that somebody was in my place. They knew where to find my dog tags and used our wedding china, one of the few things salvaged from the fire. I had to contact Casey Dolan.

Still no sign of Pete or the Captain. Several people gathered around the victim's mother. I made my way through the crowd, "Mrs. Le, I'm sorry for your loss." I offered her my handkerchief.

She wiped her eyes and held my hand, but her large bracelet got tangled in my fingers.

Sanoe turned to Mrs. Le, "The police will need to interview you, but not tonight."

The woman continued to cry into my handkerchief while the attendants loaded the young woman's body into the ambulance. When the Captain and Pete returned, they said to meet them late tomorrow afternoon as this case was a priority. I offered to stay and help interview the suspects ignoring what happened four thousand miles away. "It could have been anyone here."

"Or an accidental drowning maybe?" Pete added.

"How could that be?" I reminded him, "She wasn't wet and her clothes were completely dry."

When the party broke up, I was surprised only a few people were asked to come to the station tomorrow.

The Captain flicked his cigar onto the grass and stubbed it out with the toe of his shoe, "We'll deal with it tomorrow," and walked into the house.

Sanoe introduced her boyfriend. A nice looking guy with muddled ears. "This is Bear."

We shook hands. His grip was strong, "You box?" I asked.

"I wrestled, but that was many moons ago," he replied.

"From your size and build, Flyweight, I'm guessing?"

He nodded. "You got a pretty good eye. You a trainer?"

"Me? Nah. When I was in the Corps, I did a little boxing."

"We'll have to talk more later." Sanoe took my elbow

and dragged me away.

"My Uncle wants to meet with you late tomorrow afternoon. I'll pick you up about two." I nodded and watched her walk away on her boyfriend's arm. He didn't seem too attentive. Maybe my comments pumped his ego back up.

It was almost three in the morning when Pete managed to get me to my hotel. I called Dolan at home. It was just before midnight in L.A., but Casey was still up.

"I'll get over to your place right now and call you back."

I thanked him and hung up. What was going on? And what did any of this have to do with the Carrington kid? I pulled back the drapes to let in a breeze while a Gecko scattered along the wall. I decided to keep the window open. I'd have to live with the Geckos, even though everyone promised they didn't bite. I poured some coffee so I'd be alert when the phone rang. It did, yet it still startled me. Dolan was at my place. "Nothing seemed out of the ordinary except for your teacup and saucer on the table with your dog tags hanging over the rim."

"It must've happened soon after we left for the airport yesterday."

"They needed to get in there..." I began.

"I see," Dolan interrupted. "Travel time... makes sense. The door locks and windows look untouched. They must have picked the lock."

"Whoever it was spent some time there to find my dog tags. I recovered those and a few other mementos after the fire and put them in a foot locker." I could picture the foot

88

locker in the window seat under the window. The last time I looked there was about a year ago. "Did you look in the closets and under the cushions of the window seat?"

"Gee Sky, your closets are a mess. They're a jumble of boxes and are completely out of order."

"Did you check the window seat?"

Silence, "No, want me to go look there now?

"Yeah."

I waited, and listened to his shoes on the hardwood floors.

"That's a mess, too. Stuff thrown around, boxes overturned and jammed inside. Are you always that messy?"

"Are you kidding? I was in the Marines. Everything was stowed and shipshape. Sorted in boxes and sealed. They were stacked in an orderly manner."

"Well, whoever it was had to have spent several hours going through your stuff."

I wanted the LAPD called in to take fingerprints but I knew if the crooks were that good, they had to have worn gloves. Probably too smart to leave fingerprints.

"How did they know where to find your dog tags, Sky?"

"I haven't laid eyes on them for years, I have no idea... This is B.S., I need to come home."

"Now Skylar, you'll do nothing of the sort. Let me handle this. I'll go by your place a couple times a day and ask your neighbors if they saw anything. Besides, there's nothing you can do now. They already know what y'have."

"Good idea talking to the neighbors."

89

I hung up and took a deep breath. Someone knows where I live and where I am right now.

I laid in bed about to doze off when I sat up, "My Uncle?" Sanoe is the Captain's niece? That's another thing I thought only existed in Hollywood... nepotism.

Chapter Twelve

Last night I didn't eat much, so it was no wonder I woke up hungry. Down the block I found a little dive. Sanoe was alone at the counter, reading the paper. I didn't bother to ask and slid onto the stool next to her.

She gave me a dimpled smile and a cheery, "Good morning."

We moved to a booth, "So, how you doing? Those photos on the body must've been upsetting, yah?"

I nodded, "I called my partner long distance and he checked my place. Can't tell where they broke in."

"Sounds like professionals. Any idea who?"

Leland Morehead's warning came to mind, "Yeah, I've got a pretty good idea."

I calmed down before my blood boiled, "Sanoe, talk to me about anything but this case."

She told me she was born in Honolulu, and took a sip of her coffee.

"I fell in love with a Navy man from San Francisco, but my father said he would disown me if I married a sailor. So we waited until after he was discharged, got married and moved to D.C."

"Was he a police officer too?"

She nodded.

"Sounds like you two were doing what you loved."

She shrugged, "A couple of years later he got killed by a sniper while he was out on a phony kidnapping call. It was a mob hit, I'm sure. Some Don wanted to make a name for himself, so he had a cop killed... only that cop was my husband. After that I came back home, but the PD here was very slow to give women decent jobs. So... here I am."

"I'm sorry for your loss. I lost my wife and daughter three years ago."

We sat in silence for a while. I knew it was the shared experience of losing a loved one to violence that made it a spiritual kind of bond.

"Is Captain Liu really your Uncle?" I thought that might get us back on track.

"That was the only way I could get into police work...at first it was on the side."

The waitress came over to us. Sanoe finished her coffee and ordered something in Hawaiian, I guessed, but I had no idea what they said. My pride got the better of me. I closed my menu and said, "Same for me." Then I gave both of them my biggest smile.

Sanoe went on, "Family is very important to me. When I got home, I cared for my father and mother. My older brother was killed in the Philippines during the big war. My parents were all I had until two years ago when my mother passed, and last year, my father."

Her sadness was clear, but she didn't seem lonely. A beauty like her must have a bunch of guys lapping at her feet.

Our breakfast arrived. I couldn't believe what was on our plates. It looked like a fried egg on top of a slice of Spam on a hamburger patty, on top of two scoops of rice. The whole thing was covered with what looked like brown gravy.

I stared at her while she dug in with her knife and fork,

"What's wrong? I thought you were hungry."

"I'm sorry," I pushed my plate away and looked at Sanoe, "Is this a joke on the tourist?"

"What joke?" she took another bite. "This is Loco Moco, a traditional island breakfast, lunch, or dinner - whenever you want... Go ahead. Eat up, you'll like it."

I took some bites of the separate items, but couldn't bring myself to just dig in like she did. It was really good. Who'd have thought to put all these things together?

"So, now you know about me - what's your story? How did a hotshot LAPD detective end up working as a PI in Hawaii?"

I told her about Claire and my little Ellie. She was more interested in my TV show and movie stunt work, but I didn't bore her with all the legal stuff.

"You miss your family very much, yah?"

I guess I wore my feelings on my sleeve when it came to Claire and Ellie."

"I see you twirling your wedding ring around your finger. Interesting that you still wear it." She took another bite, "Look Drake, I've been assigned to babysit you while you're here. Nothing personal, but I hate this. I didn't train and work hard to do this shit. Captain's orders. No offense to you, okay?"

After I finished most of my Loco Moco, we headed to Chewy's last known residence on the island.

The brilliant morning sun disappeared behind dark clouds. Outside it looked like a sunset though it was almost lunch time. As we headed along the coast, the sky opened up with raindrops that sounded like pebbles hitting her windshield. She turned and looked at me, "Is that suit all you have?"

"Hey, I'm working and a guy's got to maintain a professional demeanor." The truth is I was sweating and she didn't have air conditioning in the car. The humidity and rain were going to ruin my only suit.

I loosened my tie. She took a hard left and pulled into the parking lot of Liberty House department store. "Come with me." She opened my door and pointed to the store entrance.

The revolving doors deposited us into an air conditioned paradise. Large signs hung from the ceilings, *The Future of Writing is Here. Try the NEW Ball Point Pen.* Ball point pens? Must be new in Hawaii. I followed her downstairs to the men's department. The clerk recognized Sanoe, "Aloha, Sistah," and gave her a kiss on each cheek. "Back so soon?"

"Aloha Mindy. I need to buy some shirts for this guy, maybe three or four and trousers."

The stout woman led us to a rack of colorful shirts. "Pick what you like sir." She trotted off to visit with Sanoe.

At the cash register, Sanoe took a shirt and one pair of pants out of the bag, "Here. You go change now." Even though I felt like I was shopping with my wife, I felt more comfortable right away.

On the way back to the car I asked, "You shop there often?"

"You bet. It's the nicest store in Honolulu."

We drove out of the city through lush green hills and stopped across the street from a dilapidated, single story cottage overgrown with all sorts of tropical plants. Barely

94

visible through all the foliage a, *For Sale* sign poked out at a weird angle.

"Why was a rich kid like Otis Carrington living in a dump like this? I thought his Aunt Marion was paying his bills." Sanoe stepped over old newspapers and trash that had collected on the walk.

"This house has been abandoned for some time Mr. Drake. As you can see, the condition is pretty bad." She stopped at the front door. "I must warn you, the people around here say it's haunted."

What is she talking about? Since when are there ghosts in Hawaii? "What do you mean haunted?"

"People around here stay away because it is *Kapu* to them - forbidden."

With all the broken windows and the front porch ready to collapse, she didn't have to tell me that. The whole place was probably a smorgasbord for termites, roaches and who knows. I stopped judging for a second and could imagine a young family with children and toys scattered on the lawn. She pushed the door open and led me through the dark living room. The damp stench of mildew and mold permeated the house, but with imagination, one could tell it was once a nice home. When I took out my pen light for a better look, big cockroaches scurried across the creaking floor and into cracks in the baseboard. Chirping geckos were everywhere.

Sanoe looked up at the ceiling and all around, "We've been through this place twice with a fine toothed comb...nothing. As far as we know, Otis lived here with his parents and little sister until the car accident that took their

95

lives. He was the only one who survived."

That matched what the Carringtons said before I left L.A. "Is it true that little Otis was found wandering the hills?"

"Yes, they careened off the Pali Highway and crashed. It was theorized that Otis was thrown out of the car before it tumbled over the side. They figure he was alone for maybe, two days before people saw him wandering in the forest along the highway. He was just a keiki, too young to show them where the car was or explain what happened. He was shipped off to the mainland and the house was held in trust for him. He left his home as a child and came back as a young man."

We spied one of the neighbors watching us from his yard and navigated toward him. The old man turned to walk away but Sanoe said something to him in Hawaiian. He stopped and she walked with him to his door. I wished I knew what they were talking about. Without a word Sanoe returned and we went back to the car.

I got in and closed the door. She was about to put the key in the ignition, but I grabbed her hand.

"Well? What did he say?"

"I'll tell you later", and tried to pull her hand away.

"No, I want to know!"

"Not here. We'll go to the beach and talk there."

She didn't say much on the way down to the water. I guessed she was still steamed at me for grabbing her hand. We were on a different part of the island, the East side. She parked in a dirt lot by a beach park. "You need to get a pair of shorts while you're here."

"Don't change the subject."

96

I took the ignition key out of the lock. "Well?"

"The neighbor's name is Ben Keahi. He said he was clipping his bushes one day when he noticed three people standing at the back door, two men and a woman. The house had been abandoned for about six months. They just stood there, not moving. Mr. Keahi said he yelled, 'Nobody home.' but they just stood there. Thinking they didn't hear him, he said again, 'Hey, nobody don't live der.' He said he put his cutters down to go talk to them when they suddenly appeared behind him. He said none of them had arms or legs. He yelled and they disappeared, poof."

She paused.

"Are you telling me those were ghosts? He's an old man and that was what, fourteen years ago?"

Sanoe looked straight ahead. "I'm just telling you what he said. Why would he lie?"

"You don't believe in that stuff, do you?"

"Strange stuff happens in the islands. Locals believe what they want. Our culture is full of stories we don't understand."

I couldn't believe what she'd just said. "I'd heard about the bogey man and spooks all my life, but I never believed any of it."

She then told me a story about the hairpin turn on the Nuu'anu Pali highway where Otis's parents and little sister died and left him an orphan. "A long time ago, a doctor built a big house near the highway. One night, a neighbor woman was murdered by two escaped prisoners. Some people say that when you drive by that spot, you can hear her screaming for her life. It's so scary some drivers panic and they crash their cars."

I looked at her. She was serious. "I find it hard to believe that an educated woman like you is sucked in by those stories."

Sanoe shrugged. "I have to get you to the precinct," and held out her hand for the keys.

She drove back to the city along the same winding Pali Highway. When we reached the place where the Carrington car went over the side, she slowed and pointed out the spot.

"It's a narrow, sharp S-turn. No wonder... poor little Chewy."

Chapter Thirteen

When we arrived, Sanoe introduced Dr. Leong, the Honolulu County Coroner. He stood over the body of Mai Le, "The victim was poisoned." Dr Leong was a young man of Chinese descent. "Actually, the poison caused her tongue to swell which cut off her breathing. She died of asphyxiation."

I pointed to the deep wounds on her forehead and chest where the Polaroids were nailed to her body, "Were those post mortem?"

"Most probably." Dr. Leong replied.

I looked at the poor girl and thought of several quicker, more humane ways to die.

The doctor held up a small vial.

"Athurium sap. We found it in her system."

I didn't get it. "Isn't that the weird, waxy red flower they sell at the airport?"

He nodded, "The whole plant is poisonous and can cause severe irritation and swelling of the mouth. If ingested, the sap can be fatal. We also found a considerable amount of Bourbon and opium in her gut." He held up one of the victim's hands, "see the broken fingernails?" There were chips of wood underneath. "Looks like she was scratching some kind of wood, and with the amount of opium we found in her system... she must've been pretty out of it. It would've been easy to feed her the poisonous flower sap." He tucked her hand back under the sheet, "She had to have died between twelve and twenty-four hours ago.

Sanoe considered Dr. Leong's comments, "Someone must have put it in her drink. Could it have happened at the party?"

He shook his head, "I doubt it, though it depends on how long she was at the house." He turned her body to the side. "We also found this." A spider tattoo was on the base of her neck.

"We found the same on Otis Carrington and our John Doe in L.A."

We all turned at the sound of the door opening.

It was Mai's mother.

"What are you doing in here?" Sanoe blocked her way. I couldn't believe they let her in. This wouldn't happen in L.A.

The Captain joined us a few minutes later.

"Mrs. Le," Dr. Leong bowed slightly.

"I was asked here to positively identify her body,"

Dr. Leong asked, "Are you ready for this?"

"Who else but a mother should be here?"

He pulled back the sheet. The woman bent forward and softly caressed Mai's face. She traced her fingers down Mai's cheek then she nodded and straightened up. Silent tears had run down her face and onto her clothes. The Captain put his arm around her shoulder and escorted her out of the room.

Sanoe and Pete clasped their hands in front of them and left. I followed them into the hall.

"I was thinking," Sanoe said, "Could someone be trying to distract us from the investigation?"

"Maybe it had nothing to do with Chewy. They might

have wanted to warn me..." I stopped myself. They didn't need to know about my lawsuits.

After I got into Sanoe's car I remarked, "The girl's mother was sure quiet about the whole thing."

"We all grieve in our own way."

As Sanoe and I left, I saw Pete in an animated discussion with a very tall, thin woman in the parking lot. Her back was turned to me but she was tall for a lady. She turned slightly and I got a glimpse of what I thought was ...gold lipstick? I guess Pete liked them tall and...odd.

I decided to go back to the hotel bar. I had to get the dead girl, the Polaroids and the break-in at my place out of my head.

Later, I headed back to the Atlantis Bar. Hotel Street looked very different after dark on a Saturday night, neon signs buzzed along the grungy street. The smell hit me in the face the minute I got off the bus. No mistaking what this was... the red light district, popular with sailors of all nationalities. I passed by a dance hall with a jukebox displayed in the window where three sailors, sweating in their whites rolled out the door and puked right in front of me. As I continued west, little local women tried to sell me flowers and souvenirs. As I got close to the middle of the district, some of the parking meters were draped with flower leis. The mixture of puke, and urine overwhelmed the aroma of flowers.

I found the Atlantis Bar and went inside. It was packed. Loud, drunken sailors from Pearl Harbor lined the walls of the room watching the Airmen from Bellows Air Force Base dance with the girls. I could smell trouble brewing right away. The hookers were busy tonight, disappearing behind the curtains to the back rooms. I had the feeling that sweet smoke I smelled was opium.

I recognized Bear at a table with two hookers showing a lot of cash. He was supposed to be Sanoe's lover boy. I wonder how she'd feel about seeing him like this. He was drunk, smoking a hookah and enjoying the attention from the girls when I walked up to his table.

"Hey," I kicked the chair.

"What the hell buddy? Get your own girls."

I kicked the chair out from under him. He fell back on his head. The girls giggled. I pointed a thumb, "Okay girls, go."

They grabbed his pipe, took a long drag on dreamland, before rubbing against me on their way through the beaded curtains. I pulled Bear off the floor by his collar and threw him into the chair.

"What's your problem Pal?"

"Right now, it's you."

He spit at me and got to his feet, "What the f... what do you want?"

"What was your relationship with Mai Le?"

He sat back down, scratched his head and smoothed back his hair, "Who?"

I kicked the chair again, sending him onto his back. I stood with one foot in his stomach and the other on his throat. "You know, if you don't come clean, I can always shift my weight over to your throat."

He gagged and struggled to breathe, I got off and let

102

him puke on the floor. When he was done I threw him onto a wooden chair in the corner. "Ready to talk now?"

Mitt showed up with his crowbar and four more guys as big as him, "You got any questions, you ask me." I was outweighed and outnumbered so I stood back with both my hands up, "Okay," I nodded toward the back, "your room?"

He pointed his crowbar and motioned me to go. We walked across the dance floor, through the doorway and down the smoked filled hall to the storeroom. He shoved me onto a chair knocking down several cans of Spam. The other guys blocked any chance to get out. Mitt handed his crowbar to one of the guys and crossed his arms.

"Okay, Drake. What you want?"

"Mai Le, you know her?"

"Why?"

"Curious."

"You know about the dog, so stop asking."

"Dog?" I had to think... dog? "What dog?"

He stood with both his arms crossed.

"The girl was poisoned. Her mother is grieving. I need to find her killer."

He laughed. "Yea sure, I get it... grieving mother and all dat."

That was callous. I decided to change my strategy. "You remember Otis Carrington, aka Chewy?"

"Yea. So what?"

"He's dead. Got killed in L.A."

That was news to him, I could tell by the way his fat face twitched that he didn't know.

"How he got dead?"

"Pete didn't tell you? Somebody poked him with a bangstick, him and another guy. Boom. Dead. Same way. Same place. What do you know about it"

He glared at me like I did it. "Who da other guy?" He bowed his head.

I shrugged, "I don't know. Maybe friends?"

"Da other boy had to be Rocky, Rocky Ali'i. Ya, they was friend."

"He have family?"

"Who Rocky? No, he orphan."

"So, nobody missed him?"

"They buried in L.A.?"

"Not yet."

"You go, don't come back."

I headed for the door, but I planned on coming back. In the hall, five sailors lined up to block my way. "You guys have a beef with somebody?" I clenched my fists.

"You," one said.

"I don't want any trouble. I was just going," and moved toward the door.

"Yeah, well, it's too late for that pal," he threw his cigarette on the floor and crushed it with his shoe. "Get him."

I got ready for a pounding and crouched low, fists up to guard my face. Behind me I heard, "Hey!" It was Mitt with his trusty crowbar in hand and the other four big Hawaiians.

"Dis not a even fight. You pick one guy only to fight him," he pointed his finger at me.

The sailors stopped in their tracks.

One guy pushed his sleeves up and stepped toward me.

104

He'd had a little too much "courage in a bottle," and this was a fight he couldn't win - until he reached in his hip pocket and pulled a knife. Mitt leaned in and knocked the knife out of his hand with the crowbar, "Hey, no weapons allowed in dis fight."

The sailor rushed me, his fist connected with my jaw. The force of his punch spun me around. I landed face first on the beer soaked bar floor. I was in agony from the force of his punch. When I got my senses back, I looked up to see him standing over me smiling. His brass knuckles gleamed. I kicked out with my left foot and caught him in the ankle. Something cracked. He stopped. I used my right to kick his kneecap then up to his groin. He doubled over, giving me time to get on my feet. I took two steps and punched him in the stomach just under his ribs. He let out a loud shriek and went down. I rubbed my jaw and wiped my bleeding lip. The rest of them picked up their buddy.

Mitt shook his head, "Dat's what happens when you cheat," he laughed and held my jaw in his huge hand. "Wow, you tough," turning my face side to side. "I bettah not make you too mad." He paused, "noting broken, you be okay."

"Sorry Mitt. I wasn't planning to hurt him badly, but he had brass knuckles and he deserved what he got."

The big Hawaiians escorted them into the street, I followed. "Better get him to the infirmary," I yelled after them.

Mitt nodded toward the group. "Look - dey run away like cockroaches." The sailors scurried down the street carrying their injured buddy.

I looked at Mitt and put my hand out to thank him. No response. I punched him on the arm instead.

"What fo dat?" He waved the crowbar in front of me, "I didn't saw noting," and went back inside Atlantis.

The walk back to the bus stop continued to be an education in human gluttony though there were a few couples holding hands with wilted leis dropping pink petals along the grungy sidewalk.

Chapter Fourteen

Someone banged on my door and woke me up way too early. For a tropical paradise, this place has been impossible to get a good night's sleep. I was having a great dream of spending an afternoon with Claire and Ellie. Reality can be pretty harsh as I learned when I tried to get out of bed. My face hurt, my arms hurt. Actually, everything hurt. I threw on my shirt and pants, "Just a minute!" I shouted. The pain made getting dressed take longer than normal. The clock on the nightstand read 9:30 am. How did it get to be so late?

After I buttoned up my shirt, I opened the door to a lovely woman in a big, pink brimmed hat and sunglasses. "I'm sorry if I disturbed you, I'm Ligaya. Mai Le was my daughter." She extended her hand.

I shook it, she had a firm grip. I didn't recognize her.

She surveyed my face and looked past me around the room, "Oh, I woke you Mr. Drake. I'm so sorry, but I need to speak with you." She paused, "Are you all right Mr. Drake? You look...ill."

I nodded.

"Very well, could you meet me for brunch in the dining room in half an hour? Please."

"Sure," I nodded and closed the door. After painfully undressing again, I stood under a hot shower and let the warmth relax my muscles.

Ligaya was sitting outside on the hotel's lanai with her

hat off, sunglasses pulled up in her shiny blue-black hair. Her skin was the color of cinnamon, bright white teeth with ruby red lips. The hat and sunglasses had hidden the beauty I now saw.

She gracefully gestured that I should sit. "Mr. Drake. Thank you again for meeting with me on such short notice." She looked out at the ocean, "Lovely island morning, isn't it?"

"Your name is rather unusual, Mrs. Le. What does Ligaya mean?"

"It is Tagalog for giggly or happy. I hope you don't mind, but I went ahead and ordered the buffet for us. This is Hawaii's finest brunch."

Her charm bracelet rattled when she moved her arm. "Beautiful charm bracelet. Is it an heirloom?"

"Sort of," fingering the charms. "My father gave it to me when I was young. Every year after that on my birthday my mother and I shopped for charms. It holds lots of memories from before the war."

She was right about the buffet. It was enormous. I'd never had seafood for brunch and it was delicious.

"You must try the breadfruit, it's good for you.

"You mentioned you wanted to talk to me?"

"Yes, Mr. Drake, please..."

"Call me Sky."

"Sky," she nodded. "My daughter and I escaped Manila before the Japanese invasion, so we were one of the lucky few. We came here to have a better life and live in freedom. Mai was only five when we left and I struggled to raise her by myself. When she got mixed up with this Chewy, or Otis Carrington, I disapproved. I was very

108

verbal about this which caused a large riff in our relationship." She had tears in her eyes. "Oh dear, I wish I had not been so adamant with her. I don't know what happened to Otis and it was so tragic that his life was cut short at such a young age." She paused out of respect. "But I need to know what happened to Mai. She was all I had." She crossed her hands over her heart, "Can you help me? I'm able to pay you. I don't have much but I think I can cover your fee."

"You don't feel the police can help?"

"No, they don't care about Asians here. We are just a nuisance to them. If Mai was a white girl, they would be on it like a fly."

I pulled out a small pad and took notes.

"Why didn't you approve of her relationship with Chewy?"

"He was not right for Mai. She is...was too young, only twenty, and a little immature for her age. He took her to Hilo several times by boat. Sometimes they were gone for ten days at a time. She never told me what she was doing, but as a mother I suspected the worst for a young innocent girl. Do you have a daughter?"

The question stabbed at my heart, I gave a slight nod. There was no need to go into my life story.

"So, you can understand why I was worried sick every time she went away with him. I was young once, I understand. Even when I tried talking to both of them, they wouldn't listen. I had no idea what trouble Mai was getting into at his hands."

I was hypnotized by her large, dark eyes and had to

keep reminding myself to listen.

"When I heard about the opium in Mai's blood I knew it was something Otis must have been into. The police refused to help. They said they were too busy to watch after stray girls and it was my job to keep her safe. I tried Mr. Drake, I really tried."

My heart went out to her. I couldn't stop thinking how I would've felt if my little Ellen had gotten mixed up with bad company.

She reached over and put her hand on mine, "I don't trust the police and you shouldn't either."

Slowly I pulled my hand back, "I'll need something more to go on. Do you remember anything Chewy or Mai may have said about their trips to Hilo?'

"The name of the boat was *Blue Moon*. I believe he bought it about a year or so ago. And I do remember Mai mentioning Hilo several times."

I jotted down the name, "I'll see what I can do, but I can't promise anything. My commitment is to my current client. I'm trying to learn who was responsible for the death of Otis. But if I should find anything that leads to Mai, I'll keep you posted."

"I appreciate anything you can learn." She gave me her card and asked to meet again next week, "I'd like to stay in contact with you regarding this. Is that all right?"

I nodded. She signaled the waitress and paid the check, then placed a stack of bills in my hand. "Consider this a partial payment."

As we left the table she slipped her arm in mine and we walked through the lobby to the street. I turned to go back into the hotel, but she tugged my arm. "Come, enjoy the lovely morning with me a little longer." We walked along the park. She was right again, the entire morning had been pleasant.

I helped her onto the bus. She waved through the window as it drove off. I could easily fall for an exotic woman like her, and her name doesn't end in "y".

~~~~~~~~~~

I'd been in Hawaii for two full days and decided to check in with Casey for a progress report. I'd set up a account at an Western Union telegraph office near the precinct and sent him a wire. A Sunday walk to Kapiolani Park at the end of Waikiki was just the thing to clear my head. I was surprised to find a band playing and people lounging around the lawn. The temperature had gone up, so I sat in the shade of a Banyan tree and listened for a while. The music was pretty much the same as I would've heard at a park in L.A. When I'd cooled off, I took the bus back. Along the way something kept bothering me. The LAPD was a problem, but I had the feeling I couldn't trust the Akau Kaona Police Department either. I walked past my hotel to the harbor and looked for a boat named Blue Moon. No one I asked ever heard of it. Back at the hotel, I stopped in the lobby and grabbed a map for the island of Hawaii. I might need to go there.

Chapter Fifteen

I bought a pair of swim trunks in the gift shop, changed in my room, and headed to the sand. I walked along the edge of the water next to the sea of brown skinned people with great bodies sprawled out on the beach. Bikini's were plentiful and apparently women have no problem showing off their navels here! After sticking my toe in the water a couple of times, I finally jumped into the warm surf. I swam out a few yards and noticed I could still see the bottom. It was clear as glass. I floated around for a while before I went back to my towel. The hotel had seen fit to have waiters on the sand passing out cool drinks. I took a Mai Tai off his tray. It came in a tall glass with fruit and a paper umbrella. I took a sip and realized that every Mai Tai I'd had in L.A. was just colored water compared to what they served here. It had a kick. A couple more sips and I felt pretty relaxed.

"So..." a voice echoed in my left ear, "Remember me?"

I looked around, "Miss Du Forrest." She was wearing a skimpy flowered bikini.

"Oh please. Call me Vanessa, Mr. Drake."

"Then you call me Sky. Deal?"

I followed her to her table on the lanai in the shade of a Banyan tree. Her long, brown hair fell below the small of her back. From where I stood, she hardly looked like she was wearing anything on at all!

"Look," she pointed to the sea.

112

I had to tear my eyes away to look. People were surfing the waves.

"You're from California, do you surf Mr. Drake...Sky?"

"No, not at all. I don't even swim very well... and you?"

"Yes I do, but not very well."

Soon we were joined by Vanessa's parents. They were not dressed for the beach like we were. I stood and shook their hands.

"Nice to meet you again, Mr. Drake." I pulled out a chair for her mother. "I'm sorry we didn't get a chance to visit at the party. It was so crowded and..." she waved her hand in disgust.

"I detect an accent, where are you from?"

Vanessa chimed in, "We are originally from Paris. Fortunately, we left France for Canada just before the Nazis invaded."

Her mother added, "We studied English in Quebec, then moved to New York."

"How lucky for you to have escaped the German occupation."

I thought I'd lighten the mood. Since we were facing the ocean, I mentioned how I'd learned to sail in California and wanted to see the islands from the water, "Do any of you know where I could rent a boat?"

"Oh, for Heaven's sakes, Mr. Drake," her mother exclaimed. "We have a boat. Vanessa, why don't you take Mr. Drake out on the Blue Moon?"

Did she just say the Blue Moon?

Her father sat up straight, "Why sure. It's a sixty-foot sloop moored down at the Ala Wai Yacht Club. Drake, since you sail, the two of you should have no trouble handling her."

Within an hour we were sailing out of the harbor. It had been years since I sailed. When the sails billowed out we began to glide across the water. "You take her out often?"

"Not as often as we used to. We had a friend, Chewy Carrington. He'd maintained it for us and would take it out periodically to keep it in shape."

"Used to? Were you two dating?"

Somehow I didn't see the two of them getting along.

She was silent for a moment, "We were friends." She looked up at the mast and wrinkled her nose, "We got together once in a while but didn't really date." Vanessa corrected the course, "Haul in the port line. Let's trim her up a bit." I climbed over a couple lines and cranked the winch until the sail was drum taut. The boat picked up speed.

She bowed her head, "It's hard to believe he's gone, such a nice guy too."

"What was his relationship with Mai Le?"

"Now, they were an item. Always together, about town and all that."

"I gather her mother wasn't happy about the relationship."

"Her mother?" She stared straight ahead, "I guess."

It surprised me that she didn't know the contention between Ligaya and her daughter. I thought everyone knew.

She shrugged, "I wasn't that close to Chewy and I barely knew Mai."

"So where did Chewy take your boat when he took her out?"

"I have no idea. He got paid to care for the boat and that was that. Ask my father. He could answer these questions for you."

We were now out of the harbor, in choppy waters with some impressive swells. She set the auto pilot, reached into her bag and produced a bottle of Kahlua, "Want some? If you want glasses, there's some below in the cabin... or we can just drink it out of the bottle."

We lounged on the cushions and passed the bottle between us. Serenity. Basking in the sun and enjoying the sea, what a life! She pointed off to the right, "That's Moloka'i and Lana'i there. And that big island you see in the distance is Maui."

After finishing half a bottle of Kahlua, I was relaxed...very relaxed. Life seemed real good.

~~~~~~~~~

I came to in a stateroom below deck naked, next to a naked Vanessa. Things were fuzzy in my head. When I sat up the cabin spun out of control, but it settled down after a few blinks. I put on my pants and went topside. I had no idea where we were. We must have dropped anchor off a small island whose name I did not know. Vanessa emerged from below in a thin robe, carrying the empty Kahlua bottle.

I looked at her, "You drugged me?"

"Define drugged," she smiled and tossed the bottle

over the side.

I grabbed her by the shoulders, "Why?"

She laughed, "You Haoles are so easy."

I let go of her immediately and walked to the opposite side of the boat. My head was pounding.

"I believe you're one too." I could hear myself yelling. "Why did you drug me?"

"Yell all you want. No one will hear you." She smiled a more seductive one this time. "I didn't drug you. You just had too much Kahlua." She turned on a radio and a scratchy tune came on. She started to dance toward me, lifting her hair and twirling around with her robe flowing in the breeze. She pulled me hard into her body and wrapped her leg around mine. "How soon we forget."

I pushed her off of me, turned her around and held her hair off her shoulders, a spider tattoo. "Atlantis. Why?"

"Must you be such a pain? You were much more fun last night." She twirled her long hair around my ear.

I pulled both wrists behind her and dragged her to the stern. "You're taking us back to Honolulu now."

She turned away. I picked up the radio microphone and called "MayDay, MayDay."

"Don't." She reached for the microphone. I shoved her against the wheel. "You have five seconds to get this boat on course to Honolulu or I call Mayday until someone shows up."

I didn't want to hit her but I would if I had to. She started the motor and raised the anchor. We sailed around the island until Oahu came into view. She stopped the motor allowing the boat to rock back and forth in the swells.

116

"Look, elections are coming up for my father. Please don't ruin it for him. He's worked hard for this."

"If anybody is ruining it for him it's his wayward daughter."

Several small boats were close by and I worried we'd drift into one of them.

"Look, I don't want to hurt my father, but like a lot of people on the island, I belong to a group that doesn't want statehood. My father, however, is pushing for it. As a result, I have to participate in secret. I'm one of the few mainlanders who joined them. To show I was for real I got a tattoo on my neck. Something my parents know nothing about.

"How old are you?"

"Old enough."

"How old?"

"I'm twenty-three and bored out of my skull. My parents kept me at home for my father's political purposes. You know the family man and all that." She looked off to the horizon, "It looks good." Vanessa found a cigarette, put it in her mouth and lit it. "I wanted to go away to college. Damn, no matches. I'll be right back."

After a few minutes, I wondered why she'd been gone so long and stepped out of the wheelhouse to check on her. Just as I turned the corner to the hatchway, two towering Polynesian men stood by the opening, one had Vanessa in a half Nelson. Both carried Machetes.

I slowly put my hands in front of me, palms out, "What do you want?"

One of them held the big knife at Vanessa's throat, the

other looked me in the eye and walked quickly toward me with his Machete raised. Those things can do a lot of damage with one swipe. I veered to the left just before he lunged with his blade. He tripped and missed, but grabbed a railing to stop himself from going over the side. He pivoted and headed at me again. I rolled onto my back and struck him with a roundhouse thrust of my feet, swinging my legs toward the bow. I got his belly with my right leg, his head with my left, then pulled my legs back and kicked into his ribs with both feet with enough force to hear them crack. The momentum of my kick sent him spread eagled into the ocean.

I heard the other guy yelling and swerved to see what was happening to Vanessa. The other intruder still had her in a half nelson. With his free hand he swung the blade over her head while she struggled to keep her balance. He shoved her over the side before heading my way. The guy swung the big knife like he was clearing brush. I dodged out of his path just as his shadow blanketed me. I rolled onto my back and with both feet, kicked him in the groin with everything I had. That flipped him up, hitting his head on the side of the cabin. He managed to stay upright. In the corner of my eye, I saw Vanessa pull herself onto the boat and head for the wheelhouse. The dazed attacker grabbed me from behind. Vanessa gave the boat full throttle, throwing me and the guy with the Machete over the stern. I hit the water hard, butt first. I swam hard back to the boat and pulled myself up. I didn't want to end up as a drowning victim in the local papers. As my head cleared the edge of the deck, something pulled me back down. The guy whose ribs I broke got his arm around my waist. I hung onto a mooring cleat as the boat picked up speed. I looked down at the guy. He looked like he was trying to decide whether let go of his knife or drop it and hang on. He dropped the Machete but bit me on the back of my thigh. I winced at the pain and jerked to get him off me. He wouldn't turn me loose. I bent my knees and kicked. I got him in the belly and again in his already cracked ribs. He groaned and fell into our wake. I couldn't hold on much longer and yelled at Vanessa to slow down. She cut the throttle and helped to drag me onto the deck. I coughed up enough water for a decent highball and laid in the sun. Vanessa checked my chest, and stomach to see if I broke anything, "You're going to be bruised for a while." She rolled me over, "The back of your leg is bleeding."

"Yea, the idiot bit me."

She ripped my new trousers where he'd bit through, "Sky, that guy must eat nails for breakfast. It's deep." Vanessa went below and came back with a small first aid kit.

The rest of the trip back, I lay face down on the deck with iodine and gauze on my leg. It burned like hell.

She drove me to the emergency clinic against my will. I was too weak and in too much pain to stop her. She explained to the doctor what had happened, but left out the Machetes.

After closely examining my wound, he straightened up and looked at Vanessa, "These are human teeth marks." He laughed and bent down to look at me, "I have got to hear the rest of this story." He left the room with me exposed on the gurney.

The nurse came in shaking her head. She took a look at my injury, which happened to be very close to embarrassing, "You must be the one," and wheeled me to x-ray. Why would they x-ray a bite on my leg?

Afterward she said, "Nothing appears to be broken."

"Thank God," I exhaled.

"Except maybe your ego ya?' The nurse giggled and wheeled me back to the emergency room. The doctor had a tube of antibiotic cream, and pack of dressings. He gave Vanessa instructions on how to dress the wound. After she drove us back to my hotel. I limped to my room where I lay on the bed, face down. I hardly knew the woman but she insisted on washing and dressed my injury. The icing on my embarrassment cake was when she peeled off my pants, exposing my back side.

"Hey, easy now. That's a bit tender back there."

"Don't be a baby. You'll be okay soon enough, although you probably won't be sitting pretty tomorrow." I just wanted to close my eyes and sleep. The room was quiet, "Are you still here, Vanessa?"

"Shall I stay?"

"No, I need to be at the station in the morning." I mumbled, "Just go."

"I guess there isn't much else we could do tonight with you like that!" She winked and opened the door. Before she left she said, "I'd rather no one know about this little incident."

"You and me both... wait," I tried to lean on one elbow, unsuccessfully. "Two men tried to kill us and you don't want to report it to the police? What if they decide to come back and finish the job?"

She was silent for a moment, "Let's keep this between us until tomorrow, at least, so I can smooth things with my parents first and give them a chance to consult their attorney before anything is reported."

"Sure, why not?" There was nothing I could do tonight anyway.

"Oh, on the way in the desk clerk handed me a couple messages for you. She unfolded them and read, "This is from Sanoe Fan... *Pick you up 10:00 tomorrow. The Coroner wants to talk to us.* The other was a telegram from someone named Dolan, "*All is fine.*" She put the notes on my dresser and left. I was grateful for the peace and quiet.

<u>Chapter Sixteen</u>

After my 6 am wakeup call shocked me to consciousness, I checked in with Dolan. It was 10 am in L.A. I wanted him to run a background check on the Deforests.

"How's it going?"

"Slow," I wasn't going to tell him about the thugs on Vanessa's boat just yet.

The back of my thigh still hurt but it was manageable. I decided to walk off the pain since I couldn't sit. I limped back to the hotel in time to shower and change. When I got to the lobby, I walked out front. Sanoe was waiting in her car at the valet stand, "You look like hell."

"Yeah, I know."

"Musta been a long night, ya?"

~~~~~~~~~

Dr. Leong was already talking with the Captain Liu and Pete when we arrived. "The splinters of wood we found under both Mai Le's fingernails and toenails were coated with red sand, and chicken manure as well. The red sand proves something happened to her several hours before she was poisoned. I'm not sure how the chicken manure figures in."

"What kind of wood?" Sanoe asked.

"From a Banyan tree."

"Banyan tree?" I asked.

"Banyan trees, my friend." Captain said. "Those huge beautiful, spreading trees with roots that hang from the

122

branches."

"They're all over the islands, " Pete took a drag on his cigarette, "I'm sure you've seen the one at Iolani Palace downtown... Why, there's one right in front of your hotel!"

"However," Dr. Leong injected, "there's an organism found only in the wood from Banyan trees on the island of Moloka'i. I would suggest you start there."

Captain Liu added, "I'm not sure about Moloka'i. That organism might be limited to Moloka'i trees, but I don't have the manpower to send anyone on a wild goose chase."

"Why not?" I got the feeling this case wasn't a high priority for this guy. This was the first solid lead we've had.

"The big parade is the day after tomorrow," he interrupted. "We're expecting a lot of people and I need all available men for security, traffic and crowd control."

It didn't matter what I said, he stood his ground. "You take care of your little parade." I stood up, "I'll go work the murder investigation on Moloka'i alone," and headed to the door.

"Is that so?" Pete asked, "And how you gonna get there?"

"I'll charter a boat and a skipper."

"That's not very smart," Sanoe said. "Let me fly you there. I'm a licensed pilot."

Pete stubbed out his cigarette and coughed, "I'll go along and help."

The Captain grunted, "Nothing doing Pete. What did I just say? You stay here, I need every man. Fan, you fly Drake to Moloka'i. Drop him off at the airport and come

123

right back. I'll contact Detective Derrick Nahani. He's new to Moloka'i but he'll work out fine. That's all we can do for you right now Drake."

"So, can we get going soon? I didn't plan to spend too much time away from L.A."

"I'll make a couple calls to Moloka'i."

We headed out to Sanoe's car, Vanessa was waiting for me in the hallway.

"Mr. Drake... I mean Skylar, a minute please?"

Sanoe looked at me and eyed Vanessa. "I'll leave you two love birds and meet you outside. Just remember, this is a public place."

After I was sure Sanoe was out of earshot, I asked with as much cool as I knew how, "What's up?"

"I haven't talked to my parents about yesterday. I didn't feel they needed to know yet. May I leave it up to you to break the news to them?"

"Why?" was the only thing I could manage without losing my tempter.

"Look," she took my arm and turned towards the entrance, "I checked with some people that I know. They seem to feel the tattoos the attackers had were not from these islands. Some thought they might be from an Asian gang or secret society, transplanted here."

That was something I hadn't figured on. Did I want to get mixed up with some Chinese gang or wherever they were from? I puffed up my chest, "I can take care of myself."

"But Skylar, are you sure you want everyone to know about our indiscretion and that embarrassing injury?" I held the door.

124

She paused to put on her sunglasses, "I doubt what happened on the boat had anything to do with your cases or your work here."

"My cases? How did you know I was working on more than one investigation?"

"Simple, you wouldn't be here in the morgue if you weren't working on the Mai Le murder. And we all know about your investigation into the death of Chewy. Simple deduction."

"If I decide to pursue this, will you back up my story?"

She shrugged, "Depends on where my father is in his campaign."

"You can't deny that you were at the hospital with me last night, there were witnesses. It's documented."

She shrugged, "I suppose. By the way, how is your..." and looked down at my pant leg, "You know?" She wrinkled her nose, "See you later, Mr. Drake," then strolled out the door. When I looked back to the parking lot, Sanoe was shaking her head, I supposed, because she watched me follow Vanessa with my eyes as she walked away. I put on my sunglasses.

"What's this big parade anyway?"

Sanoe started the car and headed for the Pali Highway. "The annual celebration of Pele, the goddess of the volcanoes and creator of these islands." She pointed to a large notice tied to a tree with an illustration of the goddess Pele decked out in a straw skirt, with flames coming from her head and hair.

"What's with the little white dog?"

"The dog is part of her legend."

125

"Very interesting." I really didn't care. "Tell me about Bear, is he your boyfriend?"

"Nah, just friends. We went to high school together."

"Does he work?"

She laughed, "Are you kidding? He got money from an inheritance he got from a distant auntie. Ohana, you know."

"So what does he do with his time?"

"Owns a restaurant and bar. He bought it with his auntie's money."

"Ohana? I heard that word, what's it mean?"

"Ohana means family and is very important to us. We protect our family, all of them... you know, sisters, brothers, cousins, aunts, uncles, everybody, and they protect you. They never disappoint you."

We stopped at my hotel to pack. "You won't be but a few days in Moloka'i so don't bother checking out. Meet me in two hours at the Kailua airport."

I called Western Union and asked if they had an office on Moloka'i. He gave me the address.

I took the bus to the Kailua Airport on the opposite side of the island. Lucky me!

On the way I dropped by Ligaya's place, The Pacific Island Club. I thought she ran a more classy act than this. The hostess was a pretty young Asian girl. She looked to be around twenty-one. I asked for Ligaya, sat back, drank my scotch and admired the Tiki hut decor. Bamboo, palms and flowers were everywhere. Several men in Air Force uniforms were at the bar, eating pickled, hard-boiled eggs with their beer. Second time I saw someone doing that. I took a deep breath. Luckily the place had open windows,

126

the breeze blew in the smell of flowers.

Ligaya sat across the table in a form fitting dress with a charming band of flowers in her hair. "Mr. Drake, how nice of you to stop by, and what amazing blue eyes you have - and long eyelashes. That is so wasted on a man."

"And a classy doll like you is wasted in a dump like this."

She batted her eyes, "You have great dimples."

"Thanks, I was born with them but I get the feeling you choose to be here."

"I'm so sorry to have embarrassed you Mr. Drake," she folded her hands on her lap. "I tend to say what's on my mind and it gets me into many scrapes. Please, accept my apology."

"I wanted to let you know I'll be off the island for...well, I don't know how long."

"Oh dear, you are not going to the mainland, and leaving me with so much discontent?"

"No, I will be on Moloka'i for a bit. I'll be back soon I hope. I haven't found anything about Mai's murder but I haven't had time to look into it with much earnest. I will though." I was tempted to give back her money. I was so focused on telling her I didn't do much for her daughter when I noticed a horrified look in her eyes.

"Trust me Mrs. Le I promise I'll get back as soon as I can, or I'll return your money."

She took a deep breath, "Yes, of course. I hope you will be able to find something for my poor Mai."

My promises didn't appear to comfort her. I reached across the table for her arm, "I promise. Don't worry,

127

something will be resolved."

She looked down at the floor. "Thank you Mr. Drake. I look forward to seeing you when you return. Please don't disappoint me."

~~~~~~~~~

When I arrived at the Kailua Sky Ranch, Sanoe was standing next to a new Cessna 195. I climbed in. It was a bit snug for someone my size. She got in and started the engine. I buckled up while it idled.

"Looks like we have pretty good weather."

She put on her headphones and pointed out the windscreen at clouds gathering on the horizon.

"Is bad weather coming in?" I asked, "Do you think we should wait?"

She shook her head and gunned the engine. "The weather in the islands is seldom clear all day." After she checked all items on the preflight list she looked at me, "Here we go."

We started to move and bounced down the grass strip. As we picked up speed She smiled and pulled back on the yoke. The plane lifted off the grass. She banked to the right and headed out over the water. As we climbed up through the clouds the air bumped us around like a marshmallow in hot cocoa. Along the way Sanoe struggled with the winds that whipped around the Pali until we got to clear air over the open ocean, "There is usually turbulence over the Kaiwi Channel. Its crosswinds are brutal to little planes like this one."

When Moloka'i came into view, I asked, "What's that large patch of red dirt?"

Sanoe was concentrating on not crashing our little kite

of an airplane, "Later Drake, later." She glanced over at me, "You wanna help?"

"What can I do?"

"Grab that yoke and help me hold the plane steady in this crosswind!"

Our landing was scarier than the takeoff. The wind howled across the field from our left. Together we muscled the controls and put the plane down on the dirt runway with a thump. After we rolled to a stop, we jumped out and tied the plane down with ropes attached to the ground. The bite on my thigh ached and my neck hurt from the jostling we took in the air. "Captain Liu wants me back ASAP. I'll take you to Nahani, have lunch and head back to Kailua."

"In this weather?" She paused, "It should blow through soon," and motioned me to follow her. "No big deal." My shoes and socks were covered with red mud from the landing field. Sanoe said it was from the iron in the dirt. Quite frankly I thought it was rather colorful.

Chapter Seventeen

We walked a half mile to the main road and caught the bus to the Police Station in Kaunakakai. The driver stopped in front of a rusty old shack set back off the dirt road in the shade of some trees. I asked, "How much farther to the Police station?"

Sanoe pointed to the building, "We're here."

I didn't expect anything like Honolulu or even Akau Kaona, but I'd hoped for something better than the Marines provided me in Korea. Here they'd used corrugated metal siding as awnings, propped up to shade the screened windows that lined both walls of the building. Inside, a half height wall formed the office of Detective Derrick Nahani. A large metal cage that I assumed was their holding cell filled the rest of the area behind the short wall. As we approached, Sanoe whispered, "Derrick's a young Hawaiian guy, just four months out of the academy."

"In other words he's VERY new."

She didn't respond.

I was right, all smiles. He introduced himself to me with a handshake, then kissed Sanoe on both cheeks. "I'm very grateful to the Captain for this opportunity. It would've taken years for me to attain a position like this if I was on Oahu."

"Isn't that the County Seal of Maui on the wall? Isn't this Moloka'i?

"We are part of Maui County." Nahani explained, "Our department is too small to be independent."

130

Yup. He was very new, young, inexperienced and way too eager to please...Sanoe, that is. It took a while to get his attention off her and focused on the investigation.

I gave him a quick rundown of the case, showed him the L.A. crime scene photos and explained what led us to Moloka'i.

"Anything I can do to help - you let me know," he then showed us a map of the island and the populated areas. "Better for you to stay away from the north side of the island and Kalaupapa. The town is quarantined."

"Oh yeah, I've heard about the Leper colony there."

"There are very few infected people now. A vaccine was developed during the war and only those who refused the vaccine are still a problem, but it's kapu." Derrick went on to describe the middle of the island where there used to be a sugar plantation and mill. "It's pretty deserted now overgrown and abandoned for some time. Then the main city is here," pointing to Kaunakakai on the map. "It's a small town, some mom and pop stores, a couple of family-owned restaurants, a tiny hotel, school, and one gas station." Derrick turned to Sanoe and told her how much he missed Honolulu. "The people are nice over here, but it gets pretty lonely."

We heard rain smacking the metal roof and watched the awnings rattle as the wind picked up. "I better not fly until this passes." Sanoe called the captain and told him she was stuck until she got better weather. I could hear him yelling as Sanoe held the phone away from her ear. He was not happy. She yelled back, "It's not safe to fly, period. You want me to get dead? I'm the pilot and I make the final

131

decision." She hung up.

"Okay, so tell us some more," I said

"We don't have too many paved roads. Most of my patrols outside of the city are on horseback. Hope you know how to ride," Nahani said.

"Where would you suggest we begin?" I asked.

Nahani thought for a minute, "How about the Mill? We can meet with Miss Stella."

"Oh!" Sanoe asked, "Is she still here?"

"Yep, and just as sweet as ever."

A break in the storm brought out the blazing Hawaiian sun. "You have an extra mount detective?" Sanoe asked.

Nahani nodded and took us to the stables. His horse was ready to go. Sanoe threw a blanket and saddle on a tan mare. Derrick saddled a big brown horse for me. I was up on the second try. I'd done my share of riding for the studios, and they usually had a wrangler for the actors. Wished I had an ice pack for my thigh.

We rode east along the coast about an hour. The horses were accustomed to the ocean, moving deeper into the water to cool off then back onto the beach.

We headed toward the interior and arrived at the old mill property. While the fields were abandoned, sugar cane still grew through the grass and weeds. Nahani was right, the place was dilapidated and largely hidden in the overgrowth. Trees grew through the building where there was once a roof.

"The island used to be blanketed with sugar cane." Sanoe said, "When the mill closed, a mainland sugar company bought the property. Now they take the cane to Maui for processing. We'd hoped they'd reopen the mill and give us our jobs back."

Derrick looked at her, "Dis Moloka'i girl." He patted her on the head.

She giggled. "Yeah. At one time."

"No, you Moloka'i girl, always." Derrick smiled and nodded.

"So, you're from here?" I was shocked she didn't mention it.

"Born and bred." She pointed her thumb at Nahani, "Him too." He smiled.

"Do you both still have family here?"

They shook their heads, "All gone," Derrick said.

"No work, no money," Sanoe added. "No money, no food. What kind of life is that?"

To the north, away from the old mill, I spotted a large, New England style house in a thick grove of trees.

I pointed, "Anyone live there?"

"The last relative of the original owners," Derrick said, "an older woman."

"Miss Stella." Sanoe smiled.

"Come on, let's drop by and see her." He turned his horse and rode toward the house.

"The Plumeria is in bloom," Sanoe said and pointed to some bushes covered with small, white flowers.

An old lady answered the door, "My word. If it isn't my kane Derrick and wahine Sanoe." She opened the door and gave them both a big hug and kissed both cheeks.

"This is Skylar Drake, visiting from Los Angeles." I stuck out my hand to shake hers, but she seemed confused and gave me a peck on one cheek. "This is Miss Stella

Smith," Derrick looked at her, "Your ancestors built and ran the sugar mill until it closed and you're the last surviving member of your family, right?"

She nodded, "It was all started by great grandfather Horatio Smith," and escorted us to some wicker chairs on the porch before she disappeared inside.

I looked around at the isolated area, "She lives here alone?"

Sanoe nodded, "She never married. It's only her now."

Stella returned, "I have your favorite treat!"

"Banana guava pie?" Sanoe asked.

Stella added, "...and cold pineapple juice."

I must've eaten three pieces myself.

She sat back and looked at my companions, "I remember when you two came here to work on your scout merit badges. I always thought you two would end up together. After all, you seemed to be so in love then."

Sanoe shook her head, "We were really young."

"But you remember that summer, don't you?"

A smile crept across Derrick's face, Sanoe fidgeted and rolled her eyes, "Please Miss Stella, we were just kids... keikis."

"So, Miss Smith, I'm here on business." All that mush was making me uncomfortable, "Could you tell me a little about the history of this place?"

She sighed, "I really don't get out much anymore. I make it to town once a month for supplies but I haven't been out in the fields for years. The property ends with those large trees over here," she pointed down the hill, "All the way to Kalahiki Road over that way. Once the big mainland company bought the land, I was cut off. What

134

they didn't purchase, I gave to the Moloka'i Conservation Association to be left uncultivated."

I stood and looked to where she was pointing.

She waved her hand, "It's all theirs now and they can do what they want. I don't care anymore."

The sky opened up again and the intense rain made it difficult to hear. I helped her carry the dishes inside to the kitchen. She filled the sink with water and rolled up her sleeves. I spotted the same row of moles on her arm as on the dead bodies in LA. They formed a "j". When she looked my way, I pretended I hadn't seen.

I went into the hall and looked at the old photos that covered the walls. Many were starting to fade. As I moved through them I noticed pictures of workers with shovels and aprons. I looked closer, some of the men were covered in tattoos. A spider design was on one of the buildings in the photo, similar to the tattoos on the two dead men, Vanessa and Mai Le.

I went back to the kitchen, "Pardon me, Miss Smith, but who are those men in the photographs?"

"Oh my, those were fellows who worked on the plantation many years ago."

"And what is that marking on the building?"

"Oh that? It was our company's trademark."

Sanoe brought in the leftovers. Miss Stella continued, "The native people wanted to put that on the building and plant Ti bushes all around the mill and house. They seemed to think it kept away the Houka'i Po and protected them from evil spirits. I never believed those superstitions and stayed out of it." She saw us to the door and kissed

135

everyone good-bye.

Outside Sanoe said, "The Houka'i Po are also called Nightmarchers, ghosts of ancient Hawaiian warriors. They march to sacred burial grounds or sites of ancient battles at sunset and just before dawn. When people hear their chanting and drums, they run inside to avoid being seen by them. If they see you looking...you will die."

Derrick seemed to agree with her, "Several of the Smith family died tragically or disappeared without a trace. But we think maybe it was something else."

"You mean foul play? Was someone else after the sugar business here?"

Sanoe and Derrick looked at me, "No." They said in unison.

"The Nightmarchers." Detective Nahani said.

I took a step back, "You two are kidding, right? Ghosts? You're saying ghosts accounted for the deaths and disappearances of the Smith family?"

"We're not kidding. I've talked with people who live here and they saw the torches at night and heard the drums." Derrick insisted, "It's no joke Mr. Drake."

I didn't think intelligent police officers like Sanoe and Derrick would be so superstitious. Miss Smith obviously knew nothing, or she chose to play a nice old lady who baked pies. "Believe whatever you want, but I think a live person was behind those events and I'll find out who's responsible for these murders."

We rode to the far end of the cane fields. Along the way I noticed a definite change in terrain. The foliage became dense, the air more humid and the soil softer, and darker.

136

"Well this is it, the end of the Smith property. The rest of it is wild and untouched by civilization. On the other side of the hill is the ocean."

Sanoe swept her arm across the scene, "The cane fields end here and the State forest begins. All natural, and unspoiled."

I stood up in my stirrups, looked around and saw empty patches of land to the south. "I want to check out that open field."

"Nothing there Drake, just bare dirt. Besides," she looked behind us, "the sun will be setting soon. We need to be back before dark. It'll be pitch black out here."

"Or what... the Nightmarchers will get us?"

"You think this is funny? You'll see."

I was going to have to find another way to uncover what was going on over there.

Chapter Eighteen

We rode back through the sugar cane until we came upon a large clearing with a small cottage in the center. I scanned the area and noticed several shade structures scattered around the clearing. Sanoe and Derrick wanted to ride on but I insisted we stop since it was on the way back. We weren't more than ten yards from the cottage when we were greeted by a gunshot that spooked our horses. Mine reared up on its hind legs. "What the hell was that?" I jumped off my mount and hit the dirt.

Sanoe pulled out her gun. I didn't expect to get ambushed out here. This wasn't Korea.

"Put it away Sanoe, this is Momo's property," Derrick cautioned. "He's a weird old guy. Most of the time he keeps to himself and he doesn't like strangers. He has people from town work for him from time to time." He pointed off behind us, "He's got a big chicken ranch over there. You know, eggs, chickens, roosters."

A second shot went over our heads, "Doesn't he know you?"

"Sure, but he doesn't like anyone up here unless he's invited them. Then he only allows them to walk in a certain way."

"Now, that's funny, " I laughed.

"What? I don't get it." Sanoe asked as a third shot rang out.

"I mean, do you have to skip or hop the way he chooses?"

138

"Hey, it's not funny." Kahani put his finger to his lips, "Keep it down. Momo is not normal," He pointed to his head. "His two sons live in town. At least they stop by every day to make sure he's all right."

"Okay, that I can understand."

"He Kea?" Sanoe asked.

"Yeah. His real name is Morris Jacobson, but everyone calls him 'Momo" Nahani stood up and yelled, "Aloha Uncle Momo, it's me, Derrick Nahani. Can we talk for a minute?"

"Wait..." I pulled him down, "This nut is job your uncle?"

Derrick shushed me, "Not really, I'll explain later," He stood back up and yelled, "I got two friends with me."

An old man with rifle in hand, wearing a tattered t-shirt, cutoff shorts and sandals appeared from behind some bushes. Besides the gun, the first thing I noticed was his long gray beard, big nose and enormous ears. He looked like some troll from a fairy tale.

"Okay, why you not say so?" His scraggly hair stuck out from under a beat up old Chicago Cubs baseball cap, "Just walk your horses to da gate."

Sanoe pulled me aside, "We call our elders Auntie or Uncle - whether we're related or not. It's a term of respect. Use it and many doors will open for you."

"But this nut isn't even Hawaiian."

"He's lived here his whole life and he's old. Just go with it. Okay?"

Nahani was right, Momo was nuts. He kept his rifle pointed our way and met us at the gate. It was really just a bunch of branches lashed together with rope, tied to a coconut tree.

"I'm running a business here, you take my time." He stared at me, "'O wai kou inoa?"

"Huh?"

He pointed to me, "No hea mai'oe?"

"I'm sorry, but I don't speak whatever..."

Sanoe elbowed me, "He wants to know your name and where you're from. Be respectful."

I shrugged and looked back at the fruitcake. Very slowly, I replied, "Oh, forgive me Uncle Momo, my name is Skylar Drake, a private detective from Los Angeles investigating a murder. You ever hear of Otis Carrington, nickname Chewy?"

"No, never."

"How about Rocky Ali'i?"

He shook his head.

I pushed my luck and asked, "You mind if I look around? This is my first time on Moloka'i. I'd like to get the lay of the land. You know? Learn more about you and your people."

He stared at me, no response.

I stepped toward the leaning gate.

"Hey, you trespassing, fella. Stop where you at," and lowered his rifle at me.

"You got something I shouldn't see?" I asked.

"We just want to look around Uncle Momo, we don't touch nothing." Nahani said.

He turned his stare towards Sanoe. She smiled and waved, "Aloha Uncle Momo, long time no see." She kept her eyes fixed on the man with the rifle.

"Hey, I heard you was back."

She nodded.

"Come on," Momo walked ahead of us, "Stay on the gravel path only."

We followed him down the path, I happened to step off the gravel to look at a strange flower. A shot rang out. "What I say? Stay on the path," he yelled. "Next time anybody do that I shoot in the leg for trespassing."

We looked at Derrick, "The law's the law. And he'd shoot you too."

Momo walked quickly getting ahead of us as if he didn't want us to linger too long. We scrambled to catch up. He stepped onto the sagging porch and turned around. "So... now you looked around. Go."

"Wait, what are you growing in that clearing over there," I asked.

Momo's eyes focused on mine then moved slowly, stopping at each person before coming back to mine again. "Go, now," he pulled the bolt and chambered another round.

"Law's the law," Nahani said, nodding to Momo before ushering us away.

"Could we get a warrant?" I asked Sanoe, ignoring Nahani.

"The circuit judge will be here in two days. We can talk to him then."

Without much talk we walked back to the gate where we'd tied up our horses, but I could feel eyes watching us from somewhere in the brush. I swung up into my saddle, and waited for Sanoe and Derrick to follow. We heard the

141

rumble of a vehicle. I swiveled around in my saddle and saw an old blue 6x6 truck, probably Navy surplus, roaring up the hill toward us.

"Looks like Momo's boys." Nahani flagged them down. They skidded to a stop in a cloud of dust. One of them leaned out the driver's window, "Hey Derrick, I mean, Detective. What you doing up here?"

Derrick got up close and said something in Hawaiian, Sanoe listened intently. The two men nodded and spoke their turn.

Sanoe looked away, "That was a waste of time."

"What'd they say?" I was at a loss. Spanish was rough enough for me. I never had a reason to learn Hawaiian.

"No dice," Nahani shook his head. "No warrant, no more visiting."

"So we get the warrant..."

Sanoe said, "Not that easy Skylar. This is a small island. Everyone knows everybody's business. People are very sensitive and Derrick has to live and work here. He needs cooperation from the locals."

I got the small town stuff, but Nahani shouldn't let that prevent him from doing his job.

"Okay," I looked at Nahani, "If it's going to be a problem, I'll ask him for one."

"Over my dead body, mister. Not going to happen." Nahani put his hand over his side arm. "Look Drake, you're here at our discretion... as a courtesy. If you don't play nice with the local people, you're out - off the island. Got it?"

I mumbled, "So you got balls after all." Sanoe rolled her eyes at me and rode away

"What'd you say?"

"I just said nothing seems right and I was going to check out the property."

"No, not now. It's late."

"You two go," I insisted. "I'll catch up."

They laughed, "Nothing doing. You come back with us now." Nahani barked. "That's not your horse and we aren't going to spend precious man hours out here looking for you when you get lost."

"Okay then...tomorrow." I took the reins and turned my horse around. Something was screwy.

The trail back led us over the hills and along the ocean. The horses rode well along the beach. Sanoe said, "Enjoy the view Mr. Drake. You only get Hawaiian sunsets in Hawaii."

I looked up and watched as the sun quickly dropped toward the horizon. Soon it disappeared into the Pacific, burning the blue sky into steaks of orange, red and purple. It was beautiful.

We left and got a ride back to town with the young stable kid. Of course, he tried to make time with Sanoe. It was actually kind of fun watching her shut him down. Must not be enough girls on this island.

In Kaunakakai, we walked to the hotel where I'd be staying - it wasn't much more than a door next to a market. It led upstairs to a small lobby. This place was clean, not at all as well decorated as the one in Honolulu, but comfortable.

The clerk laid two room keys on the desk, "Complimentary dinner and breakfast are downstairs in the

Cafe next to the market. Show them your room key."

I took one and handed the other to Sanoe. Derrick said good night, "I'll pick you two up after lunch tomorrow."

I used the men's shower down the hall, felt human again. My watch told me it was dinner time and I was hungry. I heard Sanoe rustling around in her room, so I went next door and knocked. She opened the door, "Going to dinner?"

"Yeah, want to come?"

The evening was hot, still and thick with humidity. Since there weren't too many choices in town, we ate at the Cafe. Wouldn't you know it, they served Chinese food. It looked like Chow Mein but tasted different. Sanoe saw my face, "It's called Pancit, sort of a Hawaiian-Filipino version of Chinese noodles."

"You grew up with this scenery?"

She picked up a wad of noodles with her chopsticks, "But I'm still amazed how beautiful the islands are."

We walked to the ocean and stared at the beautiful full moon drifting above the water. As we approached the hotel, we saw people gathered at the bakery. The workers handed out donuts to everyone. Sanoe dragged me over, "The residents gather around here every night to eat, visit, gossip, compare their days, laugh and talk about their kids, the home crops, just about everything." She took a donut off the baker's tray, "Here, have a taste."

"Oh, I know what those are, malasadas." But these were small and looked like baby jelly donuts.

"Good for you," Sanoe patted me on the back, "You're trying to learn the island way." I saw Derrick. I almost didn't recognize him. He was in shorts and Aloha shirt. He

144

blended in.

He was by our side in a flash. "Hey, I didn't invite you to this, didn't think you would be interested. We do this every night. It's a tradition." Derrick kept his eyes glued on Sanoe and used his napkin to wipe the sugar off her lip. That's when I decided to leave. It was getting way too cutesy for me again.

I walked back to the hotel. When I got to my room, I found my door ajar. I was sure I closed it. Did I forget to lock it? My hand automatically went for my gun as I slowly pushed the door open. The room was dark. I kept my gun trained at the center of the room while I reached for the light switch. The window was open, the curtains flapped in the breeze. I could smell flowers, but the whole island smelled like flowers. I switched on the light and found Vanessa sitting on the edge of the bed wearing a sheer peignoir and high heels.

"I hope you don't mind," she purred, "I let myself in."

"Do you realize how dangerous it was for you to sneak into my room?" I slipped my gun into the holster. "I'm working a murder investigation and we wouldn't be having this conversation if I'd shot you."

She batted her eyes and recrossed her legs, "Oh, pffft."

"Why are you here?"

"Oh, you know... the usual. I was bored in Honolulu and my parents... political stuff."

I knew what I wanted to do with this luscious creature sitting on my bed like an hors d'oeuvre, I took a deep breath. "How'd you get here?"

"Sailed, how else could I easily sneak between islands.

145

Besides, Moloka'i is on the way to Maui," she pouted and twirled a lock of her hair.

"This may sound stupid, but what do you want?"

She stood, the belt of her thin robe fell open. She pretended to act surprised. "I have until tomorrow afternoon at three before anyone will notice I've gone. Since I had no place to stay, I thought you might have a suggestion..." her eyes drifted to the bed, "...of where I could spend the night."

As she moved toward me things heated up. Her arms around my neck and the smell of flowers made me think about the long night I would've been facing alone.

<u>Chapter Nineteen</u>

I woke up alone at dawn to the sound of roosters crowing. Apparently, Vanessa had split during the night and a million ants were crawling all over my bed. I found the ribbon they made from my open window. It looked a lot like the freeway back in L.A.

The maid came up as soon as I called. While she worked to get rid of the ants, I strapped on my gun and went down to the Cafe for breakfast.

A note was taped to the outside of my door. It was from Sanoe. *I left early this morning. The Captain wanted me back in Akau Kaona. Derrick Nahani will pick you up around three this afternoon. Enjoy the town.*

What town? There wasn't much to it. I had one of those loco moco concoctions and some coffee. Derrick wouldn't be by for six hours, so I retraced my steps from yesterday. Something was smelling fishy, and it wasn't the docks.

The businesses on the main street were still closed, it was dead. Up ahead someone or something was walking toward me. It was a stooped over, wrinkled old woman. She held out a frail hand. "Please Sir," her voice wavered. "Could you help me out with a little food or money?"

I reached in my pocket and pulled out a one, "Here, if you turn the corner, there's a little kitchen where you can get a nice meal for fifty cents. That should leave enough for lunch later."

"Mahalo sir, you are so very kind."

She turned and walked away. I called after her, "Excuse me, don't you have any family?"

She looked back at me, "No Ohana. All died in fire." She shook her head and turned the corner.

My heart hurt for her as I watched her shuffle away. I too lost everything to a fire. After a moment, I caught up with her and gave her a couple more dollars. "Here, for your weekend meals." She thanked me again and left.

The telegraph office was open, I sent Dolan a wire, *Who is Derrick Nahani? Reply to Honolulu office. Stop.*

When I got to the stables, all the horses were gone. The town ended rather abruptly so I walked along the coast until I spotted some horses in a small corral with a little house next to it. The door was open so I knocked on the wooden frame. An old man with a cane appeared.

"Aloha. May I rent one of your horses for the day? What do you charge?"

A round woman in a flowered dress joined him. They whispered to each other and shook their heads. She looked up, "No Dice Haole. We do not know you. If we give you horse, we get in trouble. Uh uh."

"Aren't these your horses? Who owns them?"

She shooed me away with her hand and pushed the door closed, but I stopped it with my foot. I hadn't done that in years. "I give you twenty dollars for one horse and saddle." I'm talking like them now. I fanned out four, five dollar bills. "Deal?" The woman put out her hand and released pressure on the door.

They whispered to each other again before the man said, "Only if my son go with you."

"Okay." I peeled off another five.

148

A teenager with long, black hair brought two horses out. I mounted mine, "You take horses, we no see you, but you break horse, or hurt boy, and we take you to jail. You got it?"

I looked at the kid, already astride his horse. How could I steal this one with the kid right beside me?

We rode side by side without talking for some time, until I asked, "You got a name?"

He nodded.

"Am I suppose to guess what it is?"

He rolled his eyes, "Bong."

"Bong, like the sound..."

"Yeah, yeah."

"Is that your real name or a nickname?"

Nothing. We rode a bit further inland.

Without looking at me he asked, "You some big movie star in Hollywood?"

"Why?"

"Detective Nahani said you work in movies when he bring his horses."

"I used to be a stunt man for the movie studios - but I'm not a movie star."

"Used to be? You jump out of building in a single bound like Superman?"

Wow, George Reeves would have a fit if he heard that. "No, I never tried to jump out a window in a tall building, but I have jumped off cliffs and cars, ridden a lot of horses, I even got set on fire once."

"Man, that's lolo!"

"Oh?"

149

"That means, like crazy, man!"

He was quiet for a while, "You rich?"

"No, Bong, I'm not rich at all."

"Why not? You famous, ya?"

"Not really Bong, not really."

"Yes you are, liar. You talk story."

As I turned and headed toward the hills I went over yesterday, Bong pulled up and stopped. "Oh No! I not go up there, dat's kapu! Y'know, ghosts and spooks."

If you didn't want people to get near your property, the best way to keep them away would be to start a rumor of ghosts and the locals would stay away. I wonder who's responsible for the stories. I continued up the hill. Bong finally followed, but lagged far behind. It wouldn't have surprised me if he took off the moment he thought I wasn't watching.

I turned around in my saddle and yelled back to Bong, "Is there another way up this hill?"

He said nothing, but gave his horse a kick and loped up to where I waited.

"I need to get to Momo's farm."

"Don't make so much noise," Bong murmured, "I know different way."

I knew that kapu stuff was a load of crap. He must've been up here before, "Okay, show me." No response, so I pulled out my wallet. "There's a dollar in it for you." He reached out his hand. I put the bill in my pocket. "When we get there."

He turned his horse around and backtracked about ten yards where he got off and pulled aside a bush, "Here."

"You take me all the way to Momo's farm. Now."

150

He got back on his horse and rode on, my horse followed as if it knew where it was going.

We trailed along a narrow shaded path between dense brush and tall palms. Speckles of sunlight struggled to make it through the tall trees and vegetation. While Bong silently led the way, a sweet syrupy aroma filled the air. Bugs seemed to be everywhere, including down my shirt and up my trousers. The kid didn't seem to be bothered by the biting bugs. He took a path off to the left, my horse followed. Through the vegetation, I saw something colorful, "Bong." I called. He stopped but didn't look back at me. I called louder, "What's that over there?" I pointed through the trees on the right.

"I don't know," he answered without even looking.

"I'm going to see what it is." I reared my horse around and headed right. Again the horse seemed to know where to go. The boy waited a few moments before following, but he kept several yards between us. We came out at the edge of a field of colorful flowers that filled the small valley and extended up the hill, millions of different colored poppies. The scent was overwhelming.

I dismounted and walked along the soft dirt between a rows of flowers. Most of the blooms were not fully opened. The smell got stronger, a mixture of sweet and mold maybe.

"Is this all part of Momo's property?"

Bong stayed on is horse, "Here," He held out a canteen, "water my Auntie put for you and me."

It tasted sweet and satisfying.

The Poppy is the State flower of California, but these

flowers weren't orange. I suspected these were opium poppies. From the size of this spread, a lot of people must work here. That had to be how Bong knew about the secret passage. I wondered if Derrick and Sanoe knew?

I got back on my horse and told Bong to take me to Momo's house. As we went along the path, a different smell was making my eyes tear. "Bong, what is that stench?"

As usual, he didn't answer. Around us I saw several shade structures made from cut off palm trees, some had tarps stretched across the tops for roofs and others had palm branches. There must have been a couple of dozen. Something that stunk was spread over the ground in the shade of each one.

"What is that?"

Silence.

I got off my horse, grabbed him by the leg, pulled him onto the ground and lifted him up by the collar. "You know what's going on here and you'd better tell me or I'll permanently re-arrange your pretty face. Now talk."

"It's chicken shit."

"What?" I shook him by the shoulders, "Are you kidding me? Why would anyone be drying chicken shit out here?"

"For fertilizer," he grunted and shrugged me off.

Suddenly I felt dizzy. I let go of Bong and fell to my knees, then black.

~~~~~~~~~

I woke up with dirt in my mouth, probably from the floor. The air was hot and still, and I felt bugs crawling all over my skin. It was dark, I couldn't see a thing. My head felt like it was squeezed in a vise. I tried to move but found my hands and ankles were tied and my gun was gone. I must have been drugged...the water! That damn kid.

The sound of drums and people talking told me I wasn't alone. The door scraped open. Someone grabbed me, jerked me to my feet and dragged me outside into the night. I must have been out all day.

The moon provided enough light to see, but I had no idea where I was. When I looked around I saw a rusting Quonset hut and forty or fifty feet away, a roaring bonfire of some kind lit up the area. Flames and burning cinders rose into the night sky illuminating a group of people in native dress. The men were bare-chested and wore a kind of wrap-around loin cloth. The women wore skirts of what looked like, banana leaves, and white long sleeved shirts. They all wore necklaces of sea shells and green leaves. Three of the men went to the platform and blew Conch shells with an eerie tone. Come to think of it, this whole thing looked a lot like a couple of bad movies I worked.

I couldn't understand a word they said to each other, I figured it was Hawaiian or Pidgin. A woman wearing a long white dress with a wreath of flowers on her head appeared holding a small white dog. She looked just like Pele on those posters I saw in Honolulu. The closer she got, the more familiar she looked. When she stepped onto the platform by the fire, all the people in the circle moved near her and there was a man who looked like that Momo nut and his two sons. Another man appeared, a short stocky one in a loin cloth wearing a large head dress. I couldn't see his face, it was covered with a mask. The woman dressed as

153

Pele began to speak. Her voice was deep, and sounded familiar. Where have I heard that voice?

I was dragged to the platform. Must have been nearly a hundred people gathered around.

The woman said, "I am Pele. Best you remember that," pointing her long black finger nails in my face. The man in the head dress stood right behind her.

I couldn't tell if Pele was a man or a women. Her hair obscured her face. What I saw was red and distorted. But it wasn't a mask, the expressions seemed too natural.

She stared into my eyes. "You Haole have entered into a place that is kapu. Tomorrow you will pay for invading our Ohana."

"Oh don't worry, I won't tell a soul. What about that guy behind you, can you trust him?"

A deep and steady scream permeated the valley. It came from the man in the headdress. "You mock me, Haole. You must pay for this." There was a finality to his message that sent chills down my back. He raised both hands, sending murmurs through the crowd.

Momo stood up and began to chant, "Spirits have been disturbed. I pray for the Gods not to take vengeance on us."

A young man approached. It was Bong, naked but for a loin cloth and his long hair pulled up in a knot on top of his head. His whole upper body was tattooed with strange markings. With a nod the two men holding me let go.

Three bald men wearing robes carrying wooden swords jumped onto the platform. Bong untied my arms and feet, "You must be taught respect." I saw a spider tattoo on the back of his neck.

I heard shuffling, then a yell by the bigger of the three

154

as he raised his weapon. Surrounded by heavy barrels on both sides with nowhere to run, I raised my arms and took a stinging hit on my right shoulder. The pain went right to the bone. The crowd roared with approval. He used some kind of Martial Arts move I hadn't seen in Japan or Korea. Pivoting past me, he raised his sword. My arm was throbbing, but I immediately spread my feet and slowly slid my left foot back for better balance. He held his position and looked at the head man.

The leader held up one arm. My attacker lowered his sword and stepped to the right keeping eye contact with me the whole time. The leader nodded to the other two. They both came at me. They had about three feet of reach and there were two of them. The only thing I had going for me was judo and street experience, I think.

One of them raced forward with his blade overhead, I faked a move to the right, he brought it down and grazed the same arm. Again the crowd cheered.

One more hit like that and I'd be out of action. Out of the corner of my eye, I saw the other one coming my way with his sword raised overhead. His movements reminded me of a banzai charge. When he got close enough I rammed him with my head and sent him crashing into the other guy who tumbled over the first. The barrels wobbled but barely moved. As the first one sprang to his feet, he started toward me. They were barefooted, I wasn't. I stomped on his foot with my shoe and swiveled my foot, grinding his toes. His mouth opened in surprise and bent over. I grabbed his sword, and jabbed him in the groin with the handle. I'd never fought anyone this big and heavy. With my left shoulder, I shoved him into the second one who just got to his feet but I almost forgot about the last guy behind me. He swung at me but I blocked with the sword, the other two were on their feet now and there was no way I'd survive another two man attack. I threw myself off the platform and onto the soft ground below. When I tried to protect my shoulder, I smashed my face against a rock. My world went into a spin and I couldn't focus on anything. Ready to pass out, I laid down only to feel strong arms grab me, wrenching my arm. I yelled in pain. They dragged me back to the tin shack and retied my hands and feet. I had to get out of there before they killed me. But I couldn't see. My arm hurt, my shoulder was starting to swell and my face felt like it was going to peel off. I swept the floor with my legs running my shoe along the edge, feeling around for something, anything to cut my ties. My shoes caught the edge of something sharp. The corrugated metal had an edge pulled out between the dirt floor and the wall. It was small but it was something. I squirmed over to the side and rubbed the ropes along the sharp edge. I felt it working. I had to work quietly because the metal made a lot of noise. Something shuffled along the outside. I could hear noises. Was someone coming to finish me tonight? Was that Bong? I ignored it and kept working at my bindings until the rope separated and eventually my hands were free, but my shoulder was in excruciating pain. The next thing I heard was the sound of a growling dog. Was it Pele's dog? I reached down and untied my legs. My head hurt when I stood, a cloud seemed to appear before me. In the cloud I saw the forms of a woman and two men all dressed in clothes from a century ago. I didn't hear them speak but in my mind one spoke, "Go to the left. Go to the left."

The door creaked open just enough for me to slip through. The ghosts or spirits, or whatever moved ahead of me. I noticed they faded away at the waist.

Chapter Twenty

I slipped through the door cradling my injured arm while flames from the bonfire jumped and danced. Everyone's attention was focused on the platform beyond the flames. I took three steps outside the door and stumbled to the left. Disoriented, I hid in some bushes under the trees. The half moon was obscured by clouds when that strange cloud reappeared.

I found some dead vines and fashioned a sling for my right arm leaving my left arm free. I moved to the left and followed the cloud. I knew it wasn't fog or smoke from the fire. Whatever it was led me out of the shack and up a hill away from the crazy people. I reached the crest and looked back. The ceremony was still going on. As I headed down the other side of the hill, I thought I heard birds singing in the darkness and another cloud appeared to my left. It wasn't as large as before but it got my attention. I heard drums beating again. They must've discovered I was gone. The weird cloud led me into a dense jungle of tangled vines and thorny bushes The moon disappeared behind tree branches making the night even darker, and the sound of the dog returned. The cloud reappeared at the bottom of the hill. But now I heard growling all around me. I took my chance, slipping all the way on the damp soil, I stumbled down the hill toward the ocean. The more I moved, the worse my arm and shoulder felt, but I couldn't stop. I remembered the mantra that kept me alive in Korea, *Just keep moving.*

I felt a few drops of rain before the sky opened up. I was sopping wet but it felt good. I lay on my back and opened my mouth for the first taste of fresh water in a day. I closed my eyes, but with the pain in my shoulder I couldn't relax. The cool mud brought nightmares of when I was pinned down and wounded in Korea. When we got back to our lines, the Navy doctors told me the rain water saved my life and those of my men. I felt cool in the mud.

The rain passed quickly. I could now smell the ocean and drifted off.

When I opened my eyes, I was laying face down. All I could see was corrugated metal - I was back in that damn tin shack. How did they find me? I pushed up but fell back into the dirt with burning pain in my right side. Sunlight streamed through gaps and holes in the metal walls. I forced myself to sit up and saw I was covered in mud and sand. Nothing made sense, the hills, growling dog, rain, the strange cloud... and now here I was, back in this hell hole. In the distance, I heard the sound of the surf and a lot of birds. Something had changed.

When I tried to stand, my legs had a different idea, I struggled to my feet and peered outside. The sling I made for my arm was gone - replaced by a belt. The dog growled again, all around me. Outside, I heard footsteps. They were back and I had to get out.

I found the door and shoved it open. Nothing looked familiar. I held my breath and tried to run, but my legs felt like concrete blocks. With all my energy, I made it to some bushes and hid, waiting for them to find me. The footsteps stopped. That wasn't good. I peered under the branches and

159

saw two pairs of legs. I was too weak and in too much in pain to fight. I looked around and found a small tree limb to use as a club. I waited for them to get close and hurled myself at them, swinging the branch like a crazy person. I think I smashed one in the knee. He went down. I swung around and caught the other on the side of the neck. Then I hobbled down the hill as fast as I could. My legs cramped but I kept moving, stumbling, falling and sometimes rolling until I got to the water's edge. I dragged myself into the ocean. My cuts and scrapes burned from the saltwater. A couple of painful breaths and under I went. I couldn't stay under the water long, the current was strong. I popped up gasping for air. I quickly scanned the area to see if anyone had followed me. My pain had turned into agony. I got out of the water and crawled onto the beach. I must've passed out again on the sand.

When I came to I was in that damn shack again, and felt like I got run over by a steamroller. This time I wasn't alone. I was on my back, and I wasn't tied up. I heard breathing. Something cool touched my forehead.

"Drake?" I recognized that voice, "Can you open your eyes?"

Sanoe and a man stood over me. She held a canteen of fresh water to my lips, sweet water, "Drink a little of this." They sat me up, "You shouldn't have tried to run," The man said.

"Who are you and where are we?"

"Don't worry," Sanoe replied, "This is Agent Hector Garcia and we're in a safe place."

While I sipped more water, Sanoe handed me

160

something to eat, "This will fill your stomach."

I sniffed at it. "What is it?"

"Taro. Eat."

Whatever it was tasted like a raw potato.

"Mind telling me what is going on here?"

"I told you not to..."

"You shouldn't have gone up there on your own," Garcia interrupted.

"Back off you two," Sanoe scolded. "We've been conducting an undercover investigation into the island's opium trade."

"Why'd you keep this from me? It could be a motive in Chewy's death."

"Look, Drake," Sanoe said, "I'm a special agent with the FBI, working undercover in the HPD. You of all people should realize I couldn't let anyone know, including you."

"The captain is also under investigation, so he couldn't know either." Garcia added. "Don't blow this for us, we've been working too long to get these people."

"Hey, I'm here to find Chewy's killer. You can count on me to keep my trap closed about your operation." I stretched my legs, "How did Mai Le figure in all this?"

"She was a key part of the opium operation, but we convinced her to inform on her boss."

I shifted my weight, "What about her mother?"

They looked at each other, "Her boss was Ligaya. She runs one of the biggest prostitution rings in the islands."

"Are you kidding me?" I felt like a green-behind-the-ears recruit... stupid.

"She isn't Mai's mother, Ligaya is a Madam and Mai

was one of her girls. She calls all of them daughters,"
Sanoe explained. "I can understand your confusion."

"It's just terminology," Garcia said.

I shook my head. How come I didn't see it? No
wonder people smirked when I sympathized with Ligaya at
the morgue. Then she came to my room, and brunch... I fell
for the whole lie. This was embarrassing. I let myself be
taken in by a pretty face on a tropical island and played for
a fool. If I was such a sucker to be taken in like that, did I
make a mistake to trust these two?

"Opium," Garcia repeated. "It's the common thread
running through all these crimes." "There are people who
believe so strongly in keeping Hawaii for Hawaiians,
they're willing to do anything to prevent statehood. Many
of their relatives actively rebelled when the U.S. annexed
the islands."

"Gee Garcia, you almost sound like one of them. They
call themselves Pele's Followers. They believe they can
fight statehood by traditional methods like the Polynesian
Gods who governed the island from the beginning."

"It sounds like a way to lure them into the opium
trade." I added.

"I wouldn't be surprised. Opium is big money now."

"I still don't get why those people who held me are so
willing to jump into the fire for the ring leaders."

"We're still following the trail up to the head of the
ring, but people need to believe..." Sanoe said, "They want
to believe in their ancestors before them."

"The whole island is in on this?"

"Mr. Drake," Garcia interrupted, "you came to Hawaii
to learn who killed Otis Carrington. It may be that the one

who calls herself Pele may have hired the killer. You have two dead men on the mainland and a dead woman here."

"Did anyone in Pele's group know that Mai was working for you?" I asked.

"Someone must have known, why else would she be killed? All is not lost. We have one more on the inside."

"Is their cover still intact?"

"We think so."

"This shack may look abandoned, but it's where we pass information and hold people at risk."

"Who's your other inside man?"

Garcia shook his head. "Uh uh, can't tell you."

<u>Chapter Twenty-One</u>

"Why? I'm leaving as soon as my work is done."

"You want me to give up our last chance to nab these crooks?" Garcia said, "I'll tell you why I'm not sharing that information with you. Our people in California tell us the LAPD found a diver's bang stick in the trunk of your car, plus small vial of opium. That ties you to the murders of Otis Carrington, Rocky Ali'i and Mai Le. Is that a good enough reason not to trust you Drake?"

"Wait a minute, what are you saying?" It dawned on me that Dolan may have tried to reach me by telegram while I've been stuck here. "I had nothing to do with... I was hired by Marion Carrington to find out who killed her nephew."

"Relax, " Garcia said, "We couldn't find any connection between you, Mai Le and the Carrington family before they hired you. The bureau office in L.A. got an anonymous tip. After examining the bang stick, they learned it didn't match the kind used here in Hawaii."

Someone is trying to frame me and I have no clue who it could be - the studio?

"Are you okay to walk?" Sanoe asked, "We have to get out of here"

"Sure, I can walk, but my right arm is killing me."

They led me past a row of trees before we reached the main road. Garcia went back to the shack to meet with the undercover contact, "You two will be okay from here".

We kept quiet as we walked, but suddenly something

164

or someone disturbed all the birds. Sanoe held her finger to her lips, "Stay here Drake," and pulled her gun.

I crouched down beside her. No way was I going to be left here unarmed. I looked around for something I could use as a weapon and found a fist-sized rock. I tried to catch up to her but she disappeared behind some bushes. I heard two shots and hit the dirt. As I crawled to where she was, I felt the cold metal of a gun barrel against my neck.

A voice said, "Drop the rock." A second guy appeared and fired a shot into the air then leveled his gun at Sanoe. "Drop your gun."

Sanoe dropped her gun, we stood and put our hands up. They tied our wrists and marched us through the thick bushes and trees, stumbling up and down hills as we went. While the men kept their guns on us, I blinked through the salty sweat running down my forehead into my eyes. Throughout the march, tiny insects flew up my nose and in my ears.

"Where's Garcia? I whispered.

"I don't know," she mumbled.

The vegetation got more dense as we went. We stopped at a small clearing.

"Well what do we have here?" a familiar voice said.

"Uncle?" Sanoe said.

"I'm trading you two for passage off this miserable rock back to China for me and my family. The FBI seems very interested in the two of you. I'm not sure why, but they'll only deal if they get you back in good condition." He snapped his fingers and some guys untied our hands. Skinny Pete and some tattooed men wearing shell necklaces were with him.

"What's this all about Pete? Don't you like the view from your office back at the station?" A big ape of a guy came around behind me and wrenched me off the ground.

"Take it easy Pal." Out of the corner of my eye I saw Pete punch Sanoe in the stomach and drag her off into the bushes. Two men followed. "A little privacy here!" Pete yelled at them.

When I get out of this, I'll teach that jerk not to sock a woman.

"What're you going to do with her?" I yelled. It tore at my gut like the night I lost Claire and Ellie. I struggled to get loose but the guy kneed me in the back.

"What do you care?" the ape said, "You'll be on a plane back to L.A. very soon."

Pete came around the bushes, lit a cigarette and nodded to the guy. The ape dragged me up a hill. My shoulder burned with pain, but there wasn't much I could do. He had a good hundred pounds on me. He dropped me next to a tree, and tossed me a canteen of water. Pete tied my wrists. I spit in his face. Pete slapped me. I thought it would have hurt more.

They turned their backs on me and started walking. They were going to leave me out here - alone. Before they walked too far, I yelled, "Hey! How am I supposed to drink this with my hands tied?"

"Not my problem Haole," Pete yelled and both kept walking.

I yelled back, "The FBI wants me in good condition, right?"

At the bottom of the hill Pete and the big buy sat in

conversation with one other.

My bindings were loose, I managed to wriggle my hands free. I took a big gulp from the canteen. The sun was merciless now and I was dripping sweat again... losing all the fluid I just drank. I hadn't eaten in two days except for whatever Sanoe gave me. There was that growling dog sound again. I shaded my eyes and scanned the area - no dog. I was hearing things.

Sanoe was in real trouble. That wasn't my imagination and I had to find out where they took her. I put the strap around my neck, positioned the canteen and crawled down the hill. I spotted Pete and the ape. Keeping low, I crawled to a place where I could hear what they were saying.

"This is just the start of a bigger battle." The ape swept his arm across the horizon and made a fist, "We keep Hawaii for our people. We lost much since da Haoles came here. First the British and their missionaries, then the Americans push their way of life down our throats. All the immigrants spoil our sacred places. The Japanese never attack us if the Americans didn't have big naval base here." He pounded his fist on his chest, "We send them all back where they come from or killed dem."

Pete got up, stretched then walked around the tree. He stopped in front of the big guy and pulled a knife. "Kulikuli!"

"What? Why I gotta shut up?" the goon yelled. "You nobody, Haole."

"I am Ali'i here, not you. You want to get arrested and end up like all those what came before you?" Pete got louder, "Then go ahead. I got mo bettah plans and you

167

better remember who is Boss". He grabbed the big guy's knife gave a quick swipe across his forearm drawing blood, but it didn't look deep enough to hurt him. Pete tossed the knife in the bushes. The other guy threw his arms up, "What you do dat fo?"

"Because you stupid, dat's what fo." Pete shouted.

I tried to get close enough to see what was going on without being spotted. They both looked up, startled by a pair of Navy jets screaming past overhead, probably on a training flight from Kaneohe, but everything about this made me feel like I was back in Korea. Without a gun, I laid flat on the ground and pressed my hands on my temples. "Keep your head down," I told myself, "Don't let them see you." In the dirt a few feet from me, I found the knife Pete had discarded. I grabbed it and scrambled back to the hill on my belly to a hollow where I rested and caught my breath. With a knife and a half full canteen, my hopes of surviving picked up. I raised up a bit to see if I could spot them when I felt someone put their hand on my shoulder and whisper, "Shhh. Stay down and be quiet, you'll give us away!"

I rolled over and whispered, "What the hell are you doing here Nahani? Have you seen Sanoe?" He peered through the brush, "It's okay, they've gone over the hill." He stood and helped me to my feet.

"I've got to find Sanoe. I saw them take her."

Derrick shook his head and motioned me to follow him. We crept around the clearing to a tent in the bushes a few yards from Momo's cottage. Nahani pointed to the tent and two guys standing out front. I cut a small slit in the back, big enough to see inside. Sanoe was laying down, her

168

clothes tattered, and her arms and legs were bruised and scraped. I pulled away and gave a thumb's up to Nahani. He nodded and threw a rock to the side. One of the guys pulled a gun and ran to see what it was. Derrick jumped the one in front of the tent and choked him out. I tore the slit wide open. She was gagged but I could see she was glad to see me. "You okay to go?"

She nodded. I cut off her gag and the cords that bound her hands and feet. She drank from the canteen. "We have to get out of here now" she whispered. I nodded and motioned for her to follow me. Derrick dragged the guard around back and smiled when Sanoe crawled out of the tent. We followed him for some time until we made our way to a rusting, dilapidated Quonset hut, overgrown with branches and leaves. Derrick knelt down and pushed some of the vegetation aside revealing a small plywood panel near one end. After we were inside, Sanoe turned to me, "How'd you find me?"

"It was Derrick. He had a hunch you were in there when he saw the guards."

"We need to get Pete out of there," She whispered, "his life is in danger."

"Why? He's calling the shots and had me tied up. He's..."

"He's an FBI agent," Derrick said. "Pete infiltrated the group on Captain Liu's orders for the department. So far, he's done a great job getting info to us. But if we don't get him out now, they'll figure out he's a Fed and kill him."

"Does Captain Liu know he's FBI?"

"We aren't sure."

I noticed a pouch by the door. I moved to pick it up.

"Put that back. Its evidence."

"What evidence?"

"Samples of the opium." They moved the wooden panel. Sanoe looked back, "Stay here and guard that pouch. We'll be right back." Derrick crawled out after her.

I was stuck with nowhere to go and no way to communicate with anyone. If I left, where would I go? I had no idea where I was.

The sound of that dog was back. I grabbed the knife. Something or someone was outside the hut. The growling stopped. I kept my eye on the pouch and crept toward the door. Outside the sun had set and that musty, sweet smell came back. I was too on edge to sleep. All my senses were on full alert, I couldn't feel fatigue or pain. I almost wished for something to happen so I'd know I was still alive.

A noise... the snap of a branch. I resumed my position by the door, pouch behind me, knife at the ready. Faint knocking or tapping. It sounded like a pattern. One tap, a pause, followed by five taps. It repeated. Maybe it was some kid goofing around outside? I waited until I heard it again and responded with two taps I waited, then echoed the one tap, a pause, followed by five taps. The two taps were returned. The wood panel moved aside. I pulled out my knife and stood ready in the dark when I heard a man's voice, "Drake?"

Chapter Twenty-Two

"Who's there?"

"Relax, it's me, Garcia." He shined a light in my direction, "How are you doing?" and tossed a penlight to me. I picked it up and tucked my knife in my belt. He held out a canteen. "Here, drink." I gulped down the cool water and spit it out. "What's in this?"

"I put sugar in the water."

While I took another drink, he took my knife out of my belt.

"Go on, drink. You needed some energy."

My throat was raw and my stomach grumbled, but the water felt good.

"Did Sanoe and Derrick make it back with Pete?"

"I don't know."

"They must've got separated. Before we head back, we'll have to find the three of them.

"Give my knife back."

Garcia didn't move. I held out my hand, "Do you give it back, or do I take it from you?"

He twirled the knife and handed it back to me by the handle, "Here, take it. I'm not going to get into it with a Marine."

He motioned for me to go with him. I hesitated and gripped the knife tightly.

"Well, come on."

I slung the strap of the opium pouch over my head and followed. I only wish I knew the plan and had a map, at the very least know what my destination was. I never liked wandering through unfamiliar terrain, whether it was in Korea or in my LAPD days.

Midnight, the full moon was straight up. It was bright enough to read by. We'd been walking for some time - listening to our surroundings when someone whacked me hard in my right leg. I went down. He jumped on my back, pushed me to the ground and grabbed the strap. He twisted it around my neck. I cut the strap with my knife. He let out a yelp. I must have slashed him in the process That's when I discovered he had a knife, too. I jabbed my knife under his ribs. He went limp. After I pulled myself loose of the dead weight, I felt something warm running down my arm. I didn't feel the cut. When I looked up, Garcia was mixing it up with two other guys. He elbowed one in the face. I took a deep breath and decided to even up the odds. I jumped in and stabbed one in the belly and twisted the blade. He went down fast. The one Garcia elbowed pulled a gun on him. He kicked it out of his hand before the goon could get off a shot. The guy took off running. Sudden silence. Garcia was on the ground bleeding from his arm. "Make a tourniquet now," his voice was shaky.

It started to rain. I dragged him under some trees, tore the other sleeve off his shirt, tied it around his arm just above the wound, and twisted it tight with a small stick. "We have to get you to get to a hospital before you bleed to death. "

I took the guns and any ammo I could find off the dead guys.

"We'll never make it with you carrying me."

172

"I can't leave you here. That guy will be back with others."

"We both have a better chance if you take off now." He pointed, "Go straight that way about a mile and turn left at the big round boulder in the middle of the path. Our safe shack is down the hill about one third of a mile. Get going."

"Here, you better keep this." I left him a revolver and several extra rounds.

"Look Sky, it takes me thirty minutes." His breathing was labored, "I figure it will take you closer to an hour. Go."

Worried he'd bleed to death, I went as quickly as I could. The torrential downpour turned everything to mud. My legs were ready to give out but at least it was downhill. I stumbled several times. Soon, the rain subsided. I heard footsteps and hid from the bright moonlight in the shadow of a banyan tree. It must've been two or three people. I checked the knife in my waistband. The sound moved away, then stopped. I jumped out with the knife in my good hand. The first one turned, grabbed my arm and pushed me face first into the mud. It felt like he was twisting it off and I dropped the knife.

"It's us Drake, calm down." I rolled over and found Derrick and Pete standing over me. Sanoe let go of my arm and picked up the knife. I sat up, covered in mud, Pete looked just as bad.

Derrick wasn't amused, "You really need to look before you decide to kill someone," Pete threw a fist full of mud at me. "I always heard you LAPD guys shot first and asked questions later."

I pointed behind me, "Garcia is back that way a bit with a tourniquet on his arm, we have to get him to a hospital."

"I saw a couple of flatbed trucks back there." Sanoe said, "Two guys were guarding them, but I'm sure we can take them.

"Garcia can't make it on his own." I told them, "He's lost a lot of blood and the tourniquet can't stay on too long. He needs medical care."

"Okay, the truck is it," Sanoe stood. "Let's go. Derrick and I will get the truck, but Drake, you hang back and keep an eye on Pete. We need him to testify."

We arrived at the edge of the clearing. I stayed back with Pete while Sanoe led the way to the trucks. Quickly and silently they took out the guards. While we watched, they rolled the truck down the hill before starting the motor. Pete and I met up with them and jumped on the back.

When we reached Garcia the sky was getting lighter with the dawn. We had to move fast. He was unconscious and his tourniquet was soaked with blood.

It started to rain again as Pete and I hoisted him onto the truck bed. Blood oozed out of his right arm. "Get the off or he'll get gangrene," Derrick yelled over the rain.

I cut it off and put pressure on the wound. His hand looked blue.

Pete kept watch with his gun while Derrick held Garcia's arm. I got in the cab.

Sanoe said, "Get in back and protect Pete."

I looked back, "He's fine. Let's go," and made sure the
174

gun I took was ready.

Pete tapped on the back window, "They're on to us. I can see headlights."

Our truck plowed through the trees, hitting branches and bushes as we went. After a few moments we came out of the trees. Three large, bare-chested men stood with their arms crossed, blocking the road. Sanoe pressed the accelerator and swerved to the right. The men jumped into the ditch on the left and started shooting. Pete and Derrick fired back. A couple of slugs ricocheted off the roof, another shattered the outside rear view mirror. The truck skidded in the mud as we roared down the hill while Sanoe tried to keep control. Derrick steadied the unconscious Garcia. The gunshots stopped and we coasted down a straight piece of road into a ditch where the truck crashed - silence. I looked at Sanoe. Her head was resting on the steering wheel, blood dripped from her face onto her lap.

"Sanoe?" I lifted her head back. She was out cold but had a strong pulse. I climbed over her and squeezed through her open window. "You guys okay?" Nothing. I crawled onto the bed. Pete was missing. Derrick was dead, shot in his back. Garcia was under him against the back of the cab. He had a weak pulse, probably from blood loss. I heard Pete, "I'm down here." He'd flown off the truck into the ditch.

"How're you doing?"

He cradled his left arm, "I think it's broken. How's Sanoe?"

"She's out cold, looks like she got cut up when her head hit the steering wheel." My voice didn't sound like me. "Garcia is the same...Nahani's dead.

The sun was up now and the heat was already bearing down on us. I took a look at the truck sitting nose down in the ditch. Pete and I were the only conscious ones. "You need to go for help Drake, I'll stay here with the others."

He was right. I was the only one that could go. I cut some branches and large leaves to camouflage the truck. All I had was a handful of mud to soothe my injuries. Pete gave me his half full canteen.

"Stay low and get to the bottom of the hill. When you get to the clearing, make every right the house by the old mill."

Pete didn't look good at all. Then I noticed a blood stain spreading around his middle. I grabbed more mud and smeared it on his belly. "Hang in there buddy. I'll be back for you."

~~~~~~~~~~

After what seemed like hours, I came upon the house by the mill, "Miss Stella?"

She came to the door, "What happened to you?"

"It's a long story."

"You were missing for three days you lazy son-of-a-gun." I blinked twice, it was Casey Dolan standing in the doorway.

"Look, I have some injured people back there in the hills that need help now."

They stared at me, "Agent Garcia needs a hospital,"

"Take my car." Stella said.

She tossed me her keys.

"What about Derrick?"

"Derrick, I'm sorry to say, was killed."

176

Stella clutched her chest and sat down, "Oh my Lord."

"I'll be back later to catch you up."

Casey followed me to the car and rode shotgun. It took three tries to crank up the big DeSoto before we could drive to where I'd left the others. Dolan helped load the wounded into the car. We put Derrick's body in the trunk. Pete directed us to the medical clinic in town.

~~~~~~~~~

Sanoe got bandaged and released. They wrapped my sprained shoulder and Garcia was in surgery. Casey brought Stella to the hospital.

"I want you to know I think you were very brave to go in with them and expose the ring leaders," Stella said, "and it wasn't even your fight."

Suddenly I saw red, they used me.

The surgery to stitch up Garcia's arm didn't take very long. I saw him wheeled to a room with his arm in a sling and an IV bottle hanging from a metal pole.

I clinched my teeth to keep my mouth shut.

I followed and watched from the doorway while the nurse helped him into a nice soft bed. After she set up his IV, she came out and closed the door.

I took a deep breath, "Can I see him?"

She patted me on the shoulder, "Let him rest a while before you go in. He's had a rough time."

What did she say? He's had a rough time? Let him rest? Like Hell! As soon as she turned the corner, I went inside.

Garcia was sitting up but very groggy. I should have come back later but I was seeing red.

"You bastard," I shoved him back down on his pillow, "You set me up...." and took a swing at him. He blocked me with his good arm and tried to get up. I pushed him back onto the bed. He pressed the call button. A couple of big orderlies pulled me off him and took me into the hall. "Sir," one of the orderlies warned with his hand gripping my sore shoulder, "You'll have to leave the hospital now or I'll have you arrested." I shrugged him off and went out the nearest door.

I hitched a ride to the Smith place. Along the way, I figured the ghosts everyone had been seeing were meant to take advantage of the superstitious locals. I'd bet the Nightmarchers and the smoke clouds were just that, smoke screens to cover up the manufacturing and transportation of the opium on and off the island. None of these people wanted to offend the true believers, so Momo, Liu and the one they called Pele could run their operation without fear of interference from law. I stormed into the Smith house. Sanoe and Stella were having tea. The first words out of my mouth to Sanoe were, "Why the hell did you set me up?" I pointed a thumb at Dolan, "...and what the hell is my partner, who is supposed to be taking care of my business interests back in L.A. doing here?"

No one said a word.

"Well?"

"We can explain..." Sanoe said, "but we need to do this with Garcia present."

"You three better get your stories together." I warned.

The next morning Sanoe and Pete drove me and Dolan back to the hospital.

Chapter Twenty-Three

Garcia was awake, in a wheel chair waiting for us. He looked bad. I didn't care.

He took a breath, "I know why you're here, Drake."

"Well?"

"We were just about to close in on the gang," Sanoe said, "but we needed more information and Pete was our inside man."

"You were a Godsend when you showed up." Garcia said, "You made them move up their time table. I knew Sanoe would be with you and we knew it would be risky, but we thought you had all the protection you needed."

"I was your patsy. Isn't that what you're saying?" I went for him but Dolan held me back.

Sanoe said, "We didn't think Momo would figure out that Pete was undercover as quickly as he did."

"We had to get these guys and close down the poppy farm," Pete added.

"Because of your presence," Sanoe said, "we've picked up Momo and most of his followers."

Garcia got up and paced around, "After being inside, Pete didn't think old Momo was the brains behind this whole thing. It was too elaborate for him to coordinate. I suspected they were just the muscle in the machine."

I looked at Dolan, "What about you? Did you know they were using me?"

"What? Skylar Drake, are you ossified? I've only arrived here yesterday. I was concerned for your safety

179

since I hadn't heard a peep from you in days, so I contacted the FBI Honolulu bureau. They told me you were on Moloka'i. I came as soon as I could."

"Why Dolan, I'm touched."

He shook his head and waved me off, "What I really care about right now is having me a pint."

Sanoe, jumped in, "I was the one who returned Dolan's call. The Honolulu field office contacted me and I asked him to come out."

"Was all this worth the trouble?" I didn't want to be the reason their operation failed, "Did you get them all?"

"All but the leader." Sanoe replied, "He's hiding out somewhere on the windward side."

We heard a light tap on the door. Stella came in. "Momo and the boys are not behind this. Believe me, I've known them all my life. They know how to follow orders. I don't believe they've ever had an original idea in their heads." She paused. " A tall man with long red hair by the name of Kai met Momo at my house two days ago. He told Momo and me that Pete was an FBI agent."

"Who is this Kai?" I asked.

Stella replied, "A friend of Momo. A Haole from the mainland."

Pete leaned against the wall, "What else did he tell you?"

She shrugged and pointed to Garcia across the room. "Don't forget about Derrick. We lost a good man."

It was quiet for a few minutes. "Derrick had no family," Sanoe said. "I'll take care of the arrangements."

"Why would they want to kill Derrick?" Stella asked.

"They didn't. They were aiming for me." Pete

explained. "He saved my life."

I asked Sanoe, "How did you get involved with the FBI? You told me..."

"I joined the FBI when I left the islands for San Francisco. My husband," pointing to Garcia, "had joined first, then I did."

I shook my head, "Husband?"

"It was a ploy to make this operation work," Garcia said. "The agency presented the problems to us and we devised a way of infiltrating the gang, along with Pete's help."

"But we still need the head man. Is it Kai?" Sanoe folded her arms.

"Whoever it is, we can't seem to find him. He knows this island like his own backyard."

I pointed a thumb at Miss Stella, "What was her part in all this?"

"She appeared neutral while we directed our efforts on the gang. They thought they were using a kind old lady and took advantage of the situation." Sanoe smiled.

"I put one over on them, but good." Stella grinned.

Wow. The old lady had me fooled.

"You see," Stella said, "The mill was kapu for most of its working history. One by one, my family began to disappear or die. That was part of the reason the mill had to close down. The workers were scared. No one would work for us. They said we had evil spirits here. My sister was the only one who married and had children, but even she and her husband died suddenly. We don't know what happened to the children, except for Chewy."

181

"Excuse me," I interrupted, "did your family have a peculiar mark on them?"

Startled, Stella looked at me.

"Like a birthmark?"

She pulled up her sleeve, "Like this?" There was the row of small moles that made a "J".

"Exactly like that." I said, "Both bodies we found in LA had a row of moles in that exact shape."

She nodded, "Every adult in the Smith family had this row of birthmarks forming the same shape. Only on different parts of their arm, but always the arm.

"Including Otis or Chewy, and Rocky Ali'i?"

She closed her eyes and wept, "My nephews." She sighed, "My sister had three sons and a daughter. The two eldest were young when they disappeared. Otis and his sister were the youngest. I only saw them once, before the crash."

"I am sorry Miss Stella, so very sorry," Sanoe moved beside her and hugged her. "No one should have to mourn the loss of their young nephews and nieces."

"Do you know where the older boys are?" she asked me.

I felt it through my heart. "I'm, sorry. I wish I knew."

There was nothing more to say or to do in the hospital room.

Casey took my arm and lead me into the hallway. "It's best you get back to Los Angeles as soon as this investigation is completed. I learned the lawsuit with the studio maybe coming to a resolution soon. Your lawyer said the labor committee kept pressure on the studio executives and now they're about ready to take them to

182

court."

"Yeah, well my job isn't done. I still don't know who killed Chewy and Rocky." We took a walk around the hospital in silence when I remembered the job I gave him babysitting that rich kid. "Casey, I've been thinking... if you're here, who's keeping an eye on the kid you're supposed to be watching?"

"I hired someone who's better at that than I am."

"Who would that be?"

"You'll see when you get home."

"You can't make those decisions..."

"I'm a full partner, so yes, I can make *those* decisions. You were incommunicado and someone had to take charge of things."

~~~~~~~~~~

That evening at Stella's house I walked by the French doors and found Sanoe alone on the porch, staring at the crescent moon. I turned on the porch light and sat next to her.

"You're worried about Garcia."

"I have to leave tomorrow without him. Yeah, I'm concerned for his welfare."

Stella and Pete joined us. "Nice night," Stella said. "So what happened out there?"

Pete talked about what lead up to the ceremony, basically me infiltrating their "society."

"That fire and drum stuff you did, was it authentic?" I asked, "because it reminded me of a bad movie I did in Hollywood."

"We didn't have drums," Pete said.

"When I was in the hills," Sanoe said, "I heard drums too."

"This is the twentieth Century, we use Walkie Talkies." Pete replied, "We had no drums that night - none."

Stella turned pale and mumbled, "Huaka'i po."

"Nightmarchers?" Sanoe said. She looked at the moon, "It must have been Night of the Kaola."

Pete and Sanoe returned to Honolulu, I stayed two extra days per my doctor's orders. My shoulder was a concern.

~~~~~~~~~~

The twin-engine plane for our flight to Honolulu had seats that were hard and cold. I was grateful that it was a short flight. I liked first class a lot better.

Sanoe met us at the Honolulu airport. I looked at her as we walked to a waiting car. She was healing well and looked almost normal, with just a few telltale scars from her injuries. Dolan passed out in the back seat, snoring.

Even though the celebration was a week ago, Pele's posters still hung from light poles all around Honolulu. Sanoe stopped at a traffic light. Pele's costume and massive hair blocked her face.

"I've got to know - what's with the dog in the pictures of Pele"?

Sanoe pulled to the curb and pointed up at a poster. "As you can see, Madam Pele is revered and almost worshipped by the native Hawaiian people. They call her Ka'Wahine which means 'land devouring woman.' She is known for her violent temper and frequent visits to us mortals."

"Does she always have that dog with her?"

She looked at me as if I'd insulted her. "The story goes – if you are a stranger to her, she may appear as either a tall, beautiful young woman or as an old woman. I've heard she wanders up to people and tests them by begging for food or drink. Those who share with her are rewarded."

"Is this another Hawaiian legend?"

Sanoe shook her head, "People all over the world have reported seeing apparitions of an old woman at the eruptions of volcanoes from Italy to Iceland to the Americas."

I got the feeling Sanoe thought the recent eruptions and earthquakes on the Big Island must have been Pele's doing. Against my better judgment, I told her about my experiences with growling dogs, Penny at the hotel lounge and the old beggar woman in Kaunakakai that morning.

"Can you explain those as anything but Madam Pele?"

"I don't believe in ghosts and I never will."

I stared out the window and started to wonder if I'd seen her myself!

We pulled into Akau Kaona Police headquarters, Sanoe said. "Pete found out who Pele's right hand man is."

"Who?"

"I'll let him tell you."

Pete was waiting, still in bandages but he was smiling.

"So spill it. Who's the flunky doing all of Pele's dirty work?"

"He was under our nose all the time," Pete whispered.

"Okay, quit stalling and tell me."

185

"Captain Liu."

My gut tightened, "He knew you were working undercover all the time?"

"Yeah and fed me false information putting everyone of us in danger, including you." Sanoe muttered. She stared out the window and said nothing.

I followed Sanoe and Pete to Captain Liu's tiny cell. Only thing in there, besides him, was a toilet and small mattress on the floor. He was badly bruised.

Sanoe peered through the little window before opening the cell door. He laid on the mattress with one wrist shackled to the wall. When we stepped inside, he sat up. He was a mess. I could only assumed his injuries were from the arrest. Or... his own men did this to him when he was interrogated.

The Captain was brought to the interrogation room, but even after a couple hours of questioning, he still refused to tell us who was giving the orders. He was either scared to death or stupidly loyal. "If you don't tell us," Sanoe pressed him, "then you'll be charged with the murder of Derrick Nahani, opium trafficking, conspiracy, and the murders of Mai Le, Otis Carrington and Rocky Ali'i. It will all be on your head. You'll pay the penalty and bring shame to your family."

Still nothing.

Chapter Twenty-Four

I walked into the hotel bar to wait for Dolan. Pete was sitting with a woman, her back was toward me. He glanced my way and motioned for me to join them. I didn't want to interfere but decided to be polite, though I'd had enough of Pete.

"Aloha Drake, meet my cousin, Babs. She's visiting from New Orleans." Pete made several hand signs to his cousin.

The woman was way too overdone with makeup. "Please," Pete stubbed out his cigarette and gestured to the empty seat. He went on to use hand signs to communicate with her. I guessed she was deaf.

"I just told her about your investigations here and in California."

She looked familiar. I saw her at the precinct before I left for Moloka'i

She extended her hand. Even with her big sunglasses on, she had a warm, pretty smile and dimples. Her chestnut hair and long bangs covered most of her face. Actually she was completely covered with material, Chantilly lace to be precise. While all the women around us were in bare shoulders, she was covered up from her neck to her wrists. With that dress and all that makeup and hair she should have been sweltering. She had rings three deep on each finger, her arms jingled with bracelets and earrings as big as small apples.

She made a series of hand signs to Pete. He translated

187

as she signed, "I miss Los Angeles very much. The south is always hot and humid, not a place to really enjoy the outdoors."

"Why do you stay?" I asked.

Pete translated, "My husband lives there, so I do too." She excused herself and headed to the powder room.

"You'll have to excuse my cousin, she's eccentric, but I love her all the same. We grew up in L.A., then her parents died."

"Why all that lace?"

"Her husband is a minister, I forget which church. They have a strict dress code."

Dolan walked in, pulled up a chair. Babs returned and the introductions went on again. He was mesmerized by her, not sure why but he couldn't take his eyes off of her. We chatted, so to speak. Before they left she stood to shake my hand. Her three inch spiked heels made her tower over us.

"Interesting woman," I said to Dolan.

"Graceful," he replied, as he watched her leave.

It was dinner time in Honolulu. Dolan and I walked to a nice seafood restaurant. "You know, Drake, I've never been a fish lover but this comes straightaway out of the sea." I watched as he closed his eyes and savored grilled mahi-mahi and listened to the waves. When he opened them again, he pointed his fork behind me, "I think you have a friend here." I turned to see Ligaya, in a yellow and white polka dot dress, walking toward me. I smiled, hoping she wouldn't ask me about the investigation into Mai Le's death. That was Sanoe's job now.

She smiled back and put her hand on my shoulder, "Gentleman... how charming to see you here, Sky. I'm so glad you chose this place. They serve the world's best seafood."

I introduced Dolan, he stood to greet her.

"May I join you?" she asked.

Casey pulled out a chair. She noticed my scarred arms. "You should try mashed papaya and lime juice on those. When I first arrived here I found I was allergic to just about everything that touched my skin, then someone told me about papaya and lime juice. It works wonders."

I didn't let on that I knew her real relationship with Mai Le.

Dolan kept staring at her charm bracelets that clanked together like wind chimes each time she gestured.

"Well, gentleman, it was a pleasure seeing both of you... Mr. Drake, when will you be leaving?"

I looked at Dolan, "We should be out of here by tomorrow evening."

She patted my shoulder, "Be sure to stop by the club before you leave, gentlemen. Drinks are on the house," and waltzed back to her friends.

"Whoooeee. She is some lady."

"Yeah, a real lady from the old days"

"By the way," Dolan said. "I just received a telegraph from Lory."

"You've got Lory working the spoiled kid?"

"Yep, meant to tell you about that before we flew home."

"...and Marion is okay with Lory working for us?"

"Actually no," he took another bite. "She tells Marion she's playing tennis and comes to the office in her little white tennis outfit"

"Don't tell me you're dating her!"

He laughed, "No, not Lory." He paused and smiled.

"Sandy?"

He gave me a sheepish shrug.

I'm going to have to sit him down when we get home and have a little conversation about how dating clients can get us in big trouble, "So what did Lory have to say?"

"She found out that James Withers, is having financial difficulties. Apparently he has a gambling problem and lost most of his money in Las Vegas and at the track. He needed money to pay off some bookies. He was on the outs with his father just before he died. Lory suspects he may be embezzling from the Carrington family to pay off his gambling debts."

"Does Withers have any other clients?"

Casey shook his head, "None that she could find."

"I'll check it out when I get back."

~~~~~~~~~~

We sat on the lanai at the Halekulani Hotel and shared a couple of bottles of Primo as the sky lit up with another breathtaking sunset. "Boy, life can't get much better than this."

"Yes it can." Dolan said, "How about a couple drinks at Ligaya's place?"

"Maybe later. How often do you get to see a Hawaiian sunset?" We sat back and put our feet up on the short beach wall. The surf lapped at the shore while seabirds soared across the fiery sky above the blue Pacific. I was already accustomed to this and could easily forget all about L.A. A commotion behind us shattered our perfect Hawaiian evening. Mayor Du Forrest and his family strolled onto the lanai engulfed by a gaggle of reporters. In the middle of it all was Vanessa. I guess politicians are the same everywhere. It was interesting to see how the Mayor responded to the press.

"...the families of Hawaii will benefit from it." he answered. "I see a beautiful future for our islands." He smiled and spread his arms wide, "and it centers around the statehood of the Hawaiian islands." Vanessa and her mother sat quietly within picture view of him. Both women nodded once in a while and appeared dutifully interested in the subject. I caught Vanessa's eye which sparked a glimmer of recognition and winked.

"Hey," Dolan stood. "Let's get outta here. The quiet is gone and this is boring." Pointing toward the Du Forrest circus, he said, "She's not gonna break loose from that lot for some time."

My head snapped toward him, "You know about Vanessa?"

"What's to know? The way you looked at her? It's all over your face, Chum."

We slipped away and headed to the Pacific Island Club. Inside the Tiki themed place, people danced while scantily dressed women carried trays of drinks through the crowd. When we asked for Ligaya. The hostess, another pretty Asian girl, told us she hadn't arrived yet.

"Mother left instructions for us to provide for your every desire. Everything is on the house." I took a drink off a passing tray. Dolan ordered an Irish whisky from the bar. We were directed to a booth where I sat back and drank my scotch while the band played a Mambo. More people filled the dance floor until it was shoulder to shoulder. Dolan was tapping his fingers on the table in rhythm with the music when his eye caught something, "Be right back." I saw him approach a lovely woman with black hair past her waist. After a few words and smiles, he took her in his arms and danced. Claire was a great dancer but I'd always had two left feet. That wasn't bad enough to keep me out of the service but it was a definite dancing handicap. She would drag me onto the floor and dance around me while I shuffled my feet in an attempt to give the impression of dancing. It worked for her and I didn't mind.

When I saw the bottom of my glass, I had another and thought about my life before the house fire. Claire and Ellie were the glue that held me together when police work dragged my spirit into the sewers.

"Hey!" I felt somebody push my shoulder. Brushing whomever it was off me, I went back to my thoughts. "Hey Drake!" It was Dolan shaking me by the shoulders. "I'll be back in a few." He winked with the girl hanging onto him, "If you're going to hang around here and wait for Ligaya, fine, but if you decide to go back to the hotel, don't wait up." Casey had a good eye. There was a lot going on under the girl's little red dress. I raised my glass, "Enjoy." His new companion laid a big smile on me, "You lonely? I have a friend."

I'll just bet she did. I shook my head, "I'm okay, thanks."

After a while and no sign of Ligaya, I took the bus to

my hotel and wondered if I would ever set foot in Hawaii again.

It was a few minutes after midnight when I slipped my key into the door. Inside the drapes rustled with the tradewinds through the open sliding door. A figure was silhouetted against the glass. I reached for my gun.

"That isn't necessary Mr. Drake." Vanessa flicked on the table lamp.

"How do you keep getting in my rooms?"

Her well tailored look had suddenly become quite casual. "I understand you're leaving tomorrow for California."

I nodded and put my keys in my pocket, at the same time, checked to be sure my wallet was still there.

She slid up to me and pressed her body against mine in all the right places, "Well then this is the perfect time to say Aloha, don't you think?"

"Vanessa, this isn't..." a loud pop came from outside as a bullet whizzed through the open door into the far wall. I pulled her onto the floor with me. "Stay down!" I took out my gun and crawled to the patio door as four more shots echoed in the courtyard. Vanessa crawled over. "Damnit, get back," I waved her away, "Get behind the bed and keep your head down. Several more bullets crashed into the furniture and walls.

I could feel her breath on my neck, "What's happening?"

"What do you think? I said to get behind the bed!"

I pushed the drapes to the side for a better look out the patio door. Five more shots in rapid succession. They

193

seemed to be coming from the left. The hallway door flew open. Two large men burst in and aimed their pistols straight at my head. The first one shouted, "Toss you gun away, now!" The other one kept his gun on Vanessa. A third man followed them in and closed the door behind him. It was Mitt.

"Hey, when he say toss it, you do it."

I dropped my gun and pulled Vanessa next to me.

Mitt waved the barrel of his pistol at me, "Hands up and sit on bed." He pointed at Vanessa, "You ovah der." We were now on opposite sides of the bed. Mitt pulled up a chair and straddled it, but a lot of him hung off both sides. "So, you tell me, why you still here, Haole?"

"I'm flying out tomorrow."

"You, lady..." he said to her, "put you hands down now. Dat look stupid." She lowered her arms and folded them on her lap.

"Why you want to kill our dream of being our own country. Hawaii need to be for Hawaiians. No more Haoles here unless we say."

It took me several minutes to figure out what he was saying. "Did you know the money from the opium was not going to your fight against statehood?"

"What was all dat for?"

"To make Momo and the person dressed like Pele rich. It was a con."

He looked at me for a long time. "What you say? You talk story."

Vanessa said, "They were treating you like fools."

He stared at me, "So you say this thing was not for us?"

194

"No Mitt. It was to fill their pockets and convince the community to support them, not you or your people."

Mitt got up, rubbed his head and paced the room. The other two men stood frozen. "What we gonna do now?" one of them asked.

"You were a part of the distribution pipeline, weren't you? The Atlantis was probably the last stop before the drug left the island."

He nodded and continued to pace.

"Let me help you Mitt. If you decide to work with us, I can talk to the FBI."

"Listen to him, it makes sense," Vanessa added, "If you wait for the FBI to find you, they might not want to bargain."

Chapter Twenty-Five

The gunshots had emptied the hotel of guests and brought Honolulu Police officers to my room with their guns drawn. I put my hands up with everyone else and showed the first officers on the scene my P.I. license. After the commotion subsided, I made a couple of phone calls to the FBI Honolulu field office. After trying twice, someone finally returned the call. Pete took it and told us he'd meet us at the station.

"You three made the right decision," I told Mitt.

"You sure?" He said as the police handcuffed the three Hawaiians and Vanessa. "I don't feel like I did a good ting."

A Police officer said, "You can sort this out and wait for the FBI down at the station." Pete met us there. Mitt and his men weren't arrested but he was cited for discharging a firearm within the city limits.

"Thanks for not put us in the jail," Mitt said. "But we don't know who is being Pele."

The other two shrugged and shook their heads like a couple of school boys, "See? If we know we tell you," Mitt insisted.

"Pele have dat big hair," one said, "I can not tell if was he or she inside."

Pete put a cigarette in his mouth and shrugged "I have no idea."

I wondered about that myself. Pele's voice was deep and soft. It could have been a man trying to sound like a

196

women or a women trying to sound like a man.

Mitt said, "It sound like they have bad cold or someting." He turned to Pete, "You got an extra smoke?"

Pete handed him a cigarette and matches.

Allergies? I went out and paced the hallway. My mind was going a hundred miles an hour, and I knew the answer was right in front of my face. The veins in my neck were burning.

I went back inside and slammed my hand on the wall. "I've had about enough of this island and all the secrecy!"

"Hey! Dis not L.A. and you not a cop. Don't yell at me like dat."

I bent down and looked Mitt in the face, "Tell me who had Chewy killed in L.A."

He looked at the ground and wrung his big hands together, "Chewy was nice kid, him and Rocky. They shouldn't be dead."

"Then who did it?"

He looked at me with sad eyes, "Pele give da order to Momo for make them go away and Mai Le too."

"So," I asked, "Momo killed them in California?"

He shook his head, "Momo nevah leave the islands."

"Who pulled the trigger?"

"Momo know dat, not us."

"Was it his sons?"

Mitt pursed his lips and thought, "Could be. Momo trust dem. Dey his sons."

I pulled Pete aside and whispered, "I have a good idea who Pele is."

He looked at me, "You sure?" and blew a smoke ring,

"Who?"

"I can't tell you just yet. Not until I'm absolutely sure."

I told Sanoe and Pete about the graceful way Ligaya and Pele both moved their hands. The red face Pele had meant allergies.

"You'd better be right." Sanoe said. "She's the sweetheart of the precinct. The boys will not look kindly on this accusation."

"See the connection? She stayed close to the police and local FBI to keep an eye on everyone." I realize that's probably why the police ignored her operation on Hotel Street.

"Ligaya always good to me and my boys." Mitt offered, "Pretty sure she not part of opium deal."

Pete thought, "I believe Drake may be right. "I'll have her picked up...if we can find her." He flicked his cigarette butt on the floor and stepped on it.

On the way out, Mayor Du Forrest and wife exploded into the precinct. "Where's my daughter?"

I spoke briefly with them about what happened on the boat, Vanessa's tattoo and membership of the political group, Pele's Followers, to save Hawaii for the Hawaiians. They knew none of this.

"I don't believe these accusations, my daughter would never do those things." Helen insisted.

"I'm taking her home, NOW," she stood. "I want to see Captain Liu."

"Captain Liu is under arrest."

I finally got back to my room around two in the morning. Dolan was asleep on the sofa and fortunately, the hotel management didn't throw me out. However, I know Mrs. Carrington will hit the roof when she gets the repair bill for the bullet-riddled hotel room. I peeled off my sweaty clothes, showered and hit the sheets.

The telephone startled me awake at some ungodly hour of the morning and I wasn't very happy when I reached for the receiver, "What?" I bellowed.

"Ligaya is here of her own accord," Sanoe said. "Garcia and Pete are questioning her right now."

I woke Dolan, "Let's go, they've got Ligaya."

I splashed some water on my face and shoved Casey out the door with me. There Ligaya sat alone in the interview room, charming, convincing and dressed to kill. When she denied knowledge of the killings or any involvement in the opium operation, I could tell Dolan was believing her stories.

"That's all an act. That might work on some green cop back in the Hollywood Division, but I've seen too many of the same worn out tricks." I went into the room.

"Well, well. If it isn't Mr. Skylar Drake, private investigator." She crossed her legs at the ankles and sat back with one elbow over the back of the chair. "I trust you and your associate had an enjoyable evening at my establishment? My daughter told me the police were looking for me."

"Please remove your gloves and place them on the table, Ma'am."

"That sounds a bit ungrateful." Her smile disappeared

199

and a wrinkled frown appeared, "and I came here of my own accord."

I pointed to the table and repeated, "Your gloves please."

She looked at the two-way glass of the observation room where Pete and the others were. "Very well." Showing no emotion, she pulled each finger of the gloves and slowly slid them off her hands. There was no redness, swelling or welts. Just beautiful skin, graceful hands, blood red nail polish and her charm bracelet.

"... and your hat as well, please." Without a word she first withdrew two long silver hat pins and placed them on the table. Pete stepped into the room and moved them out of her reach. Ligaya stared at him. She then carefully lifted the large brimmed hat from her head, revealing her beautiful features, but there seemed to be a redness along her hairline.

Sanoe joined us in the room, "Excuse me Ma'am," she lifted Ligaya's bangs. There was a red swelling along her hairline. Pete took a couple of Polaroid photographs.

"Now, would you please push up your sleeves?"

Ligaya did as I asked. A number of small scabs along her forearm formed a design, like connect-the-dots.

Ligaya looked at her arms, turning them over and back again, "I was gardening... bougainvillea and hibiscus can be treacherous."

That was a safe answer. Most people would have accepted her explanation, but when I was at the LAPD, I'd heard every excuse in the book, and more. I thought for a minute.

"Can the FBI lab test to see if she'd recently used

papaya on her arms?"

"Sure," Sanoe said.

Ligaya was escorted to the lab in handcuffs. In the meantime, her house and businesses were searched.

Dolan and I were on the patio with a cup of ice tea. Agent Garcia stepped in, "Our guys found a costume and wig hidden in a wooden chest under a false floor panel. It looked like what you and Pete described Pele was wearing... and they were covered with red dirt."

When Ligaya was brought back into the room, Garcia fanned the photos of the get up found under the floor on the table. "Your fingerprints and traces of papaya were all over the clothes."

She stared at the two-way glass in silence, emotionless. Her charming demeanor had evaporated.

"Did you kill Otis Carrington and Rocky Ali'i?" I asked.

"No!" Ligaya looked at the floor and shook her head. She raised her tear stained face to me with those chocolate brown eyes. "I have never killed anyone."

"Did you have any knowledge of their deaths?"

No response.

"The truth is going to come out. Either now or in court."

She sat back and turned her face toward the opposite wall, "I don't have to answer any more questions. I wish to speak to my lawyer."

That was that. We wouldn't get anything more until her attorney arrived. She knew how the system worked and used it.

Pete suggested that we talk to Momo. He came in with his attorney, it was Mrs. DuForrest. That's all I needed, Vanessa's mother was representing the crazy old man?

Chapter Twenty-Six

I looked at Garcia and Sanoe, "We need something to motivate Momo and Captain Liu to give up the leader."

Garcia sat back and folded his arms. Pete was tapping his foot, and Sanoe had her head in her hands.

"There may be a way," Sanoe said.

She sat quietly and looked at Garcia. "I have something I think will work, but I need a written document that states I head the interrogation."

"Of course, why not?" spilled out of my mouth.

Pete nodded.

Garcia stared at the Sanoe and she back at him. "If you agree," she said, "I want it in writing with a lawyer present."

Garcia's eyes did not leave hers. He went back into the interrogation room and sat next to Ligaya, "Look, if you tell us who killed Otis Carrington and Rocky Ali'i, we'll guarantee your safety."

"And what makes you think I need to be protected?" Ligaya laughed.

Garcia returned, "She won't break," and looked at Sanoe.

"In writing!" Sanoe repeated staring back at Garcia. Pete's head bounced back and forth between them.

I shuddered. She needed a lawyer and a legal document to guarantee her wishes with her husband? They stared silently at each other. I didn't know what to say. Finally Garcia stood and left the room.

He came back with a young man, "This is Al Nickels, Attorney at Law," and motioned to Pete and me to follow him out of the room.

It bothered me that Sanoe didn't trust her husband, why? I looked at Garcia as we waited in the hallway. "A bit unusual, isn't it?"

He shook his head, "No, not for us. Our careers have always come first. I would do the same in her situation."

"Will this change? I mean shouldn't your spouse be the one you trust, you know, to watch your back?"

He looked at me then the wall as if he'd never thought of it.

A few minutes later, the attorney called Garcia back into the room.

After Nickels left, the two of us were invited into the conference room. "Momo and his sons are in the middle of this." Garcia was quiet, looking at his hands. He then shifted in his chair. Maybe because she got the better of him?

"First is the captain," she explained. "His men roughed him up and learned nothing. We have his family in protective custody. Captain Liu wants them protected but we can't hold them much longer."

Liu was brought in. Sanoe announced, "We have Mitt and his boys in booking. They're being charged with the Carrington, Ali'i and Mai Le murders. I'm not sure where you fit in. Your family is now safe and will be released home."

"Don't release my family, they are all in danger. Don't!"

"We have the right people, Momo and his sons." She grinned, "Auntie and the girls will be fine." She signaled the officer to take Liu downstairs.

"No - you have the wrong person!" They stood him up, "Listen to me, you have the wrong person."

Liu was shuttled out of the room. The four of us stood in the hallway watching as he struggled and screamed.

"Okay what's next?" Garcia deferred to Sanoe.

"Drake, would you like to do the honor of interrogating Ligaya?"

"My pleasure."

I sat across from her, still composed even with her arrest pending.

"I wonder why your lawyer hasn't shown up."

"I have no idea. Maybe you didn't contact him like you said you would."

"Oh, we contacted him all right, he didn't seem interested. Maybe you owe him money?"

She ignored the question and smiled, "That's impossible." She paused, "I believe I'm entitled to a court appointed lawyer. Do you have any suggestions Mr. Drake?"

"Looks like you'll spend some time in jail until we find one."

She flinched. "I don't know how that filthy costume got under my floor boards at the club. Perhaps you should interview some of my daughters. I would think that would take a great deal of time and money the police department doesn't want to spend. I wonder what public opinion would be if they knew the taxpayers paid for investigations that went nowhere and that my much loved business had to shut down."

I left the room. Pete and Sanoe were waiting for me. "You'll get nothing from her," Sanoe said. "Ligaya has some big name people interested in the longevity of her business."

"Why" They both looked at me. I didn't think about the big name clientele Ligaya serviced. She is in the entertainment business after all.

An officer poked his head in, "Captain Liu is ready to talk. They're bringing him up now."

We waited in the observation room while he was brought in.

"Keep my family away from my house. They need to be protected."

"Too late," Sanoe said, they're being driven back to your house as we speak. We're holding Mitt for extortion and operating a drug ring, and Momo and his sons for murder..."

"No, it's Ligaya. She headed the ring. Stop her! She'll kill my family."

He laid out the entire operation. Ligaya was the ring leader, he was her second in command and Mitt and his guys were their logistics people. Momo's sons were the muscle.

"Did you or Ligaya give the order to kill Mai Le, Otis Carrington and Rocky Ali'i?"

"No. Not me. I don't know about Ligaya. Momo sent his sons to Los Angeles about a week ago. I don't know why."

"Why would Momo want Carrington and Ali'i dead?"

206

Sanoe pushed a pad of paper in front of Liu, "Your statement."

Liu snatched the pen and filled three pages, "I included names and dates to make it easier for you." He signed it and pushed the pad to her. "Please keep my family safe," he begged.

Captain Liu was handcuffed and removed from the room, head down, defeated. Sanoe was standing in the hall as Liu walked by. "I see you have a little something left in your heart, Uncle." Sanoe said, "Putting me in danger deliberately with Pele's council. That was low. Whatever happened to Ohana?"

While we watched the captain being taken away, I whispered to Pete, "Why kill Carrington and Ali'i in California?"

Pete lit another cigarette, "Search me."

He took over the interrogation of Ligaya, without her lawyer. She denied everything. Ligaya ignored Pete and stared at the ceiling while he shouted questions at her. Garcia stormed into the interrogation room and ordered him to leave.

"You ordered Mai Le's murder, why? She's your girl."

Ligaya turned on the charm full strength, "Why I did nothing of the sort. She was my daughter."

"You mean your hooker, don't you, Madam Ligaya?" She said nothing.

"You were Pele, the ring leader of the opium..."

"How dare you accuse me of killing my daughter and being the leader of an opium ring! I want a lawyer now."

Garcia stared at her, then motioned for an officer.

"Throw her in the yard during male exercise. We'll see how long she lasts." Garcia sneered as she was dragged out by two male officers.

She finally lost it, "Get me a lawyer, now or I'll have your head. I know people, dangerous people."

~~~~~~~~~

I walked the corridors. The stress of the interviews was took a toll on me. I saw a fully adorned Babs walking down the hall. Again her back was to me I didn't get a chance to say hello, or however they sign it. Pete came running down the hall, "Drake. I wanted to get you before you left for the mainland."

"I'm leaving later this afternoon."

"Yes I know, my cousin, Babs..."

She walked up to us, orange lipstick and nails this time, bright orange. She smiled still pretty and sweet. Her black eye makeup and long false black eye lashes were so overdone, I couldn't see the color of her eyes. She signed to me with her orange fingers flying. Pete translated, "I need to know if you would be interested in a partner for your TV exercise show. I know people in business who may be interested in an investment."

I was surprised and somewhat speechless.

She signed again, "Are you interested?" Pete translated.

"Ah, sure. Perhaps we can talk about this more." I suddenly realized what a stupid comment that was. I was about to apologize when she continued, "I will have them contact you in L.A. One of them is there now, but he'll only be in L.A. for a few days. Perhaps you could meet before he leaves for New Orleans." Babs took a piece of paper and wrote his name. "I'll contact him. When should I tell him to call?" she signed.

Dolan is here, I'm here, I couldn't think...Lory. "I'll be back in a few days. Have him call Lory, my secretary and she will take it from there."

Pete and Babs looked at me funny, "Aren't you leaving today?" Pete asked.

"Maybe, I'm not sure."

Babs fingers went wild, "He will only be in LA for a few days more, you may miss each other if you stay," Pete translated.

"Well, we'll work it out. Thank you ma'am."

I took the paper, Paul Smith was printed on it. "I'll call Lory and have her be on alert for Mr. Smith." I pocketed the paper, nodded and headed for the Captain's office.

Chapter Twenty-Seven

The four of us were having coffee when an officer came in, "She's ready."

Garcia looked at his watch, "That didn't take long."

"Ligaya's loved by many in the department," Pete said, "She was only in the yard for five minutes when they pulled her out.

Garcia sat across from her and waited.

"I'll have your head for this," she snarled.

"Who killed Mai Le?"

She closed her eyes and breathed deep, "Kai."

"Who the hell is Kai?" Garcia yelled.

Ligaya squinted her eyes, "Our contact in L.A. He and I were at an event when we heard Bear say something odd. We went to Mae's room and looked through her things."

Garcia sat quietly.

"We learned that she planned to turn over evidence exposing the opium operation to Officer Fan at the DuForrest party. I was about to send her away immediately, to the Philippines, but Kai had other ideas."

"Mai Le knew about the murders in California?"

Ligaya nodded.

"Why leave her body at the Du Forrest party for everyone to see?"

"Kai likes to show off his work."

"Who killed Otis Carrington and Rocky Ali'i?"

No response. Garcia slid a pad of paper and pen to her. She picked up the pen.

~~~~~~~~~~

Sanoe and I watched Bear's head bob back and forth in the interrogation room.

"I'm too close to this to be effective," Sanoe whispered, and sent me in to talk to him.

"Hangover?" I asked as I sat next to him.

"What's going on here? Do I need a lawyer?"

After Bear admitted to knowing Chewy and Rocky from his bar, I asked him why the two boys went to LA.

"I think I do need a lawyer."

"Why?"

"To protect myself."

"From what?"

He looked at the two-way mirror, "From everyone."

"All I need to know is why the two of them went to L.A. That's all I want to know."

Bear looked at the table for a long time. "I can't leave until I tell you something, hey?"

"The truth would help and you can go on your merry drunken way."

He continued the silent treatment.

"I understand you're the owner of the Atlantis Lounge."

"Don't you try to use my business as leverage. I own it free and clear."

"Never doubted your business sense so to speak. I just wonder what shady things we would find if we spent time looking closely at your...business."

He glared at me.

"You know, Mitt and his boys are in custody right

now."

His jaw dropped. "Okay, you only want to know about Chewy and Rocky?"

I waited.

"They went to L.A. to visit a relative who lives and works there. Some rich guy who is, I don't know...brother, cousins or something from way back. They had birthmarks that they said all the men have, a row of freckles I think on their arm or leg, something like that.

"Was it like a "J?""

He put his head in his hands, "Yea, I think. I can't remember."

"What was the relative's name?"

He put his head back, "It was a real good name, long, odd name. Some old guy born here but lives in L.A. now."

~~~~~~~~~~

Sanoe and I went to visit Momo in his cell. We brought in chairs and sat close.

"We have signed confessions naming you and your sons in the murder of Otis Carrington, and Rocky Ali'i. Since you did not do the actual killing you'll be out in a few years, but your sons will never see the light of day. They'll be charged and convicted of two murders." I sat back and let him think about it.

"Is this what their mother would have wanted for them?" Sanoe asked.

"She was a wonderful woman." He shouted, "Keep her out of this." Momo's hands turned to fists as he lunged at Sanoe, knocking her to the floor. He grabbed her chair and threw it against the wall. I jumped the crazy old guy, grabbed him and threw him down on the mattress. He

212

kicked at me with both feet, rolled and reached for Sanoe. She grabbed his wrist but he swung at her with his other arm. She blocked it and elbowed him in the jaw. Momo shook it off and came at me swinging both arms. I punched him hard in the nose but he turned on Sanoe. She picked up her chair and held him back like a lion tamer. I got behind him and locked his right arm behind his back. Blood poured out of his nose but he kicked at both of us and screamed until two officers rushed in and put cuffs on him. Sanoe and I left to let him cool off before we made another try at getting him to talk.

When we went into the interrogation room a couple hours later, Momo was shackled and handcuffed.

"If you think so highly of their mother," Sanoe said, "you should honor her by helping your sons."

"That Liu, I never trusted him." Momo muttered, "Captain or no Captain, he has a bad spirit about him. Ligaya never would turn me or my sons over to the police."

"Who hired you to kill Carrington and Ali'i in L.A?"

Bloody from our fight, he said, "You get me a lawyer and guarantee leniency for my sons and I'll talk."

My plane was due to leave for L.A. in three hours. I called Marion Carrington and told her I was within hours of learning the whole story about Chewy's murder. She agreed to postpone my departure for two more days.

Dolan called Lory and alerted her about Paul Smith. She told him my lawsuit with the studio was filed but we still had weeks to wait.

213

~~~~~~~~~

Mrs. Helen Du Forrest walked in. Sanoe explained Momo's demands and the need for him to cooperate.

"I met with my client," Du Forrest said, "and learned the warrant and search of his house and barn resulted in nothing."

Sanoe replied, "Two other people involved with the opium ring swore that the Momo's sons killed two people. You're telling me we can get all we need from Momo if his son's get a deal?"

We waited, Du Forrest did too.

"What can you do to help us?" I finally asked.

"Nothing," Du Forrest said. "Why are you talking to me and not the DA?"

I looked at Sanoe. She stared at DuForrest, "Quebec."

The attorney sat up, "I don't like threats."

"I have a witness," gesturing to me. "I've never threatened you. Detective Drake, did you hear me threaten Mrs. Du Forrest?"

I shook my head.

Du Forrest closed her eyes.

"There is someone I would like to refer you to that can do a better job than me in a situation like this."

"I don't think so Mrs. Du Forrest."

"Yes," she leaned forward and glared, "Yes I do."

"Will this person have all the clout and information you have to make it work?" Sanoe demanded.

"I will make sure he has all the...information...he needs, Miss Fan. All of it."

"You have twenty-four hours Mrs. Du Forrest. Not a threat, simply telling you our timetable." Sanoe paused,

"I'm sure you understand."

DuForrest pushed her chair back from the table and was out of the room like a shot.

"What was all that about?" I asked just as Garcia and Pete walked in.

"Mind telling us too?" Pete asked

Sanoe smiled, "You'll see. If anything happens to me in the next twenty-four hours, check my safety deposit box in L.A.. But I doubt anything will. The DuForrests are a smart family."

~~~~~~~~~~

The next morning, Al Nickels was seated with Momo in the interrogation room "I've confirmed with my client and the D.A.'s office. They agreed with Momo's requests for his sons' leniency." He stopped to show us typewritten papers stapled together. "These are for both your sons, go right ahead," the attorney said.

I couldn't have been more shocked that the D.A. would agree to all of this, in writing no less.

"Keep in mind," Sanoe warned, "We won't sign the agreement if we don't deem the information valuable."

Momo looked at his lawyer. "Best I could do, sir. We can end this interrogation if you like. But I doubt you will get a better deal than this."

Momo nodded

"I was contacted by Kai two days before Carrington and Ali'i were killed." Momo explained, "He wanted them dead in twenty-four hours from the time of the call. He didn't tell me why. The money was good and his threats to expose me and my family were real. My sons were on the next plane to L.A. under assumed names. Kai told me if they killed them in L.A., no evidence would lead back to Hawaii and certainly not to Moloka'i. I told them to use a bang stick since people on the mainland were not that familiar with them."

"What does this Kai look like?" I asked.

"I only see him once when he pay me. The day my sons finished the job"

"And?"

"He was a regular guy, y'know... aloha shirt, big hat and shorts." He thought for a minute. "He take only one puff from his smoke, throw it out and cough."

I closed my eyes and remembered watching Withers light up a new cigarette, taking one puff before coughing and putting it out in an ashtray at the hotel.

"Why did this Kai want them killed?"

"Don't know."

"Tell me what you think, Uncle Momo," Sanoe said.

"I only tell you this for my sons."

I excused myself and called Dolan at the hotel. "Where's Withers?"

"Why?"

"Where are the Carrington girls?"

"I have no idea. Why?"

I could just picture Withers talking to Momo. My mind switched to the sincerity he showed for Chewy when we first met. Could he be after the Carrington's fortune, even marrying Marion? Was he planning to get rid of Lory and Sandy next?

"Wait for me, I'll be there in a few minutes."

I told Casey my concerns and called Lory in L.A.

216

"Have you seen Withers lately?"

"Uh, not for a few days-why?"

"He may not be who he appears to be."

Chapter Twenty-Eight

With Otis Carrington's murder solved, my assignment in Hawaii was finished. We stayed an extra day for Nahani's Funeral.

Per his request, Derrick was cremated. Casey and I joined Pete, Garcia and Sanoe on a small boat while she said a few words and poured his ashes out over the ocean. The wind picked up just as she opened the urn and he flew with the wind.

~~~~~~~~~~

I planned to fly back to L.A. with Casey. Sanoe and Garcia were on the same flight. They were to change planes in L.A. for Washington D.C. Sanoe and I relaxed with a cocktail in the airport lounge and waited for our flight to be called. "I don't know that Garcia and I can go on together. We've been miserable for three years." She confided, "We work well together, but our personal life... it's just not working."

It's hard to hear about any marriage breaking up. What I wouldn't give for a few more days with Claire.

"Is there anything you can do to work it out?"

She shook her head, "We're company people, not family people. I made a big mistake."

"Does Garcia feel the same way?"

She nodded.

Sincerely came on over Muzak. Sanoe sat back and listened for a few minutes.

"Come, let's dance." I stood and held out my hand.

She felt good in my arms. I'll always remember the fresh scent of her hair. "Sanoe, you're smart, pretty and loyal. You'll be fine."

We danced in close for the next song *Mr. Sandman,* when I felt a tap on my shoulder, "May I cut in?"

It was Garcia. I went back to our table and watched. It was easy to see they cared for each other.

A man at the next table leaned over, "Y'know, that looks like one of my movies." it was Jack Lemmon, "The other guy always gets the girl," he raised his glass. "They say life is the most interesting game anyone of us plays. *"*

I held out my hand, "Sky Drake, you and I worked on a couple of projects. I do stunt work back in L.A."

"I thought I recognized you," he smiled and returned my hand shake.

"What are you doing over here?"

"Just finished working on a film about the Navy, Robert something or other. We wrapped up shooting and I'm heading home."

"Just so you know, she's not my girl. That guy's her husband."

He let out a belly laugh that shook the table, "That's worse than anyone could have written for my characters".

~~~~~~~~~~

We landed at Los Angeles International Airport on a typical hot, smoggy afternoon. Casey and I said good-bye to Garcia and Sanoe. We watched them go hand in hand, to their connecting flight. "You know," I said to Dolan, "I think they'll be okay,"

"Yeah, maybe."

The taxi got us to the office, no need to go directly home. We waded through stacks of mail and bills. I found a letter from Mr. Morehead, the attorney handling my suit against the studio. *Your case is set for a hearing in four weeks. Contact us in preparation for your court appearance.*

I stuffed it back in the envelope, "Looks like the studio is going to meet me in court," I muttered to Dolan.

"Good, you need your day in court, and be sure to contact the newspapers. The public needs to know what they're trying to do to you."

I remembered the thugs and getting rolled down that hill. I'll bet the photo of my dog tags was their doing. The studio guys hate unfavorable stuff about them in the news. "If I can get a reporter to listen."

I opened the last envelope, this one marked *Confidential.* It contained a six page letter.

Dolan showed me a big note mixed in with the bills, *CALL ME! Lory.*

We looked at each other, and took a deep breath. Dolan said, "Lory... do we want to... I mean, now?"

I stuffed the envelope in my pocket and nodded. He picked up the phone and dialed.

~~~~~~~~~~

We managed to shave, shower and change clothes before heading to the Carrington Estate for a late dinner. I was surprised they were even speaking to us after the accusations we made about Withers. Sandy answered the door in a revealing cocktail dress. "Come in you two."

Lory was lighting the candles on the table set for five. Dolan whispered to me, "Did you know this was a formal

220

affair?"

We stood back and checked each other's attire. I shook my head, "We're good, at least we're not wearing blue jeans."

Marion was wheeled in by the butler. She was dressed in turquoise. "Gentleman, I'm grateful you could make it," extending her hand to us. "Thank you for all your help."

The meal was served with great style by the maid and a butler. "This is our farewell dinner for Otis and his friend. Their bodies were cremated yesterday. I'll bring their ashes back to Hawaii, where they wanted to be. The three of us will accompany them to their final resting place."

The maid set out goblets of pineapple ice cream covered in chocolate sauce. Marion clinked her spoon on the edge of her goblet, "This was Chewy's favorite dessert." It looked awful but tasted good.

"We wanted you two to help us celebrate their lives and accomplishments," Sandy said with a straight face.

Following dinner we were joined by Marion's new companions, Mr. Sneed, her new accountant, and Mr. Thorp her new attorney. I pulled Lory aside. "What happened to Withers?"

"After your call, Withers was immediately terminated with no explanation per your request. Auntie hired an accounting firm to look over her investments. Mr. Sneed found that Withers had been filtering money into an offshore account. We called the State Bar Association and reported him."

Marion commented, "I feared Withers was planning to

do away with the girls one at a time."

"After that," Sandy continued, "Aunt Marion decided she didn't want Withers around anymore and 'threw him to the dogs,' as she put it. These two are her new companions."

"We worried about Marion and you two." Dolan said, "Withers might have gone after you to get her fortune."

"Oh don't worry about that. Auntie has a great lawyer and accounting firm that look after her every need now."

Lory said, "You know, as boys Chewy and James Withers spent a lot of time together.

Marion added, "Those two were very close. Why would James do something like this to us. It's just not like him."

"Remember, " Sandy commented, "James was away at college. We didn't see him for quite a few years."

"After he came home," Lory added, "he was not the same person. We assumed his father's death affected him."

Chapter Twenty-Nine

We were exhausted from our flight and stopped at my place for a beer. I pulled out the fat envelope and read it. It was a report Lory had requested from the FBI. I was stunned, "Dolan!"

He looked up, "Yea?"

Dolan read the letter and stared at me. "James Withers? According to this...dental records show that skeleton the FBI have is James Withers and not Ted Stone." The driver's license picture they included looked like James Withers.

"So, who is this Withers we've been dealing with?" I asked. I closed my eyes and in my mind, I saw that fancy, fussy James Withers at the Carrington Mansion with all his little accessories. "Y'know Casey, I encountered a lot of guys like him in Hollywood. The first time I met him, I spotted the bad dye job on his hair and beard."

"Now that you say that," Dolan said, "I thought the way he was decked out was a bit much when we met him at his hotel. When he walked us out I got a flash of those huge monogrammed cuff links. It was just for a split-second and I couldn't make out all the initials, but I thought one letter could've been an ornate T."

"But at the mansion," I reminded him, "The guy's shirt cuffs were monogrammed with J.W.W."

I thought about the money Withers was embezzling.

Dolan looked at the drivers license, "*James Walter Withers* - that makes sense."

"Maybe, but a dead person doesn't come back to

life...ever.".

I read some more, "and from all the bookies listed, he's not a very good gambler. So, how was this guy able to afford a posh place like the Sunset Tower Hotel?"

Dolan muttered, "Now I'm worried about the Carringtons, three women living alone in that mansion... with Withers circling like a vulture."

My mind was still on overdrive. "Wait a minute." I thought again, "A few weeks ago the FBI came to my door about a dead stuntman... Ted Stone. I hadn't worked with him for a few years, but they had ID that said it was him. He was always a fancy dresser with a yen for champagne, women and gambling in Vegas." I wracked my brain and searched my memory, "Y'know Casey, the guy that claims to be Withers dressed a lot like Stone used to.

We stared at each other for a moment, "Nah... that's so far out in left field." We stared again. "You first," he said.

"I wonder if Withers was really Ted Stone and the body the Feds had was James Withers. But how could Stone have pulled that off... and more importantly, why?"

I crossed my arms, "Ted Stone was a stunt man. He had some bit parts in several films. He was an actor and could pull that off."

"Could he be after the inheritance of the Smith family in Hawaii as well?"

"That could've been his motive for all the hocus pocus. I learned something from Stella about a curse on the Smith family. All direct descendants of the line met with brutal deaths or disappeared. I'll bet there are still people that have taken an active role in making sure the legacy of the curse endures."

"You're telling me that several generations have been affected?"

"Otis's parents had four children. Two of the boys disappeared. His sister died in the crash with her parents and Otis was killed. As a result, when Stella dies there'll be no more direct descendants... or none that we know of."

"Why haven't they done away with Stella? It doesn't make sense."

"Search me, and we can't bring the LAPD in on this. They'd think I'd gone totally cuckoo."

"What about the FBI? After all, they're the ones with the odd body on their hands."

The beer didn't help with our fatigue, Casey passed out and I fell asleep in an easy chair. We woke up around lunch time and ordered a pizza. While we chowed down on the pie, I called the San Francisco Bureau and asked for Olivia Jahns."

They said she transferred to the San Diego bureau and gave me the number. I left a message for her to call ASAP.

We went back to the office and waited for her call. It was almost four and we were getting ready to call it a day when the phone rang.

"Is this the infamous Hollywood stuntman, Skylar Drake? As I live and breathe. How the hell are you?"

"Olivia!" Just saying her name out loud awoke memories of our time up north. "Sorry, this isn't a social call, I could use your help."

"Okay shoot," she giggled.

I tried to explained my theory, but Casey kept interrupting me to be sure I didn't forget anything, At first he got on my nerves, but thanks to him, I didn't get too distracted by Olivia.

"Who's the lead agent on the case?"

When I told her about Tanner and Miller, she replied "Oh no, numbskulls," and sighed, "Unfortunately, that's out of my jurisdiction. I wish I could help but I can't. Is there anyone left at the LAPD you can trust?"

I held my hand over the receiver, "Casey, she wants to know if there's anyone we can trust at the department."

He laughed and shook his head, "Not really."

"Try to think of someone. If I ask for a transfer it could take weeks or months."

"Well, it was good to hear your voice again. Let's get together for lunch sometime. What do you say?"

"Sure Sky. You L.A. guys are always so sincere. I'll let you know."

As soon as I hung up, Dolan snapped his fingers, "What about Nelson?"

"Do we have any other choice?"

"He's relatively new and no, we don't have any other options I can think of."

~~~~~~~~~

Casey and I strolled into LAPD headquarters around half past six that evening. Everyone was gone except for Nelson. His door was open. Inside he was toiling over a stack of paperwork.

We knocked, he looked up with blurry eyes and gave us a blank stare.

"Hello Nelson," Dolan said. "Remember us? I believe we were introduced to you as the Bobsey twins by Robbs."

"Oh...Yes... the two boys from the morgue, come in."

226

I thought he would tell us to get out, but his stare softened. "Come on in and have a seat."

His eyes were still too small for his head. I still didn't trust him and his smile seemed forced.

I let Dolan do the talking. He loved to talk and he had more patience than me. He went through the investigation and the results of the interviews with the captain, Momo and his sons and Ligaya. I simply filled in what he missed or glossed over.

We promised a report in two days, he was happy to hear that. Dolan asked if he knew anything about the Ted Stone case the FBI was working.

"You know the drill Dolan. Even if I knew anything, I couldn't tell you."

That comment ended our conversation. He didn't say anything else and he wasn't going to answer any more of our questions.

He looked at his watch, "I haven't had dinner yet." He nodded toward the stack of case files on his desk as he pushed his arm into the sleeve of his jacket. "Care to join me? I'll come back and finish this mess afterward."

We followed him to a joint around the corner while he talked about the changes he'd made in the precinct, "I'm trying to communicate more openly with the public and with my men. I've even read this book called, *How to win friends and influence people*, by Dale Carnegie. It's great and has good concepts to live by in business."

Yep. He was a college boy. He reads books that have no pictures in them.

He ate quietly for a while then looked up, "Okay,

227

suppose you two tell me why you really came by to see me."

Again we waited for each other to start.

"You guys think about it. I'll be right back," and went to the men's room.

"What do you think?" Casey asked.

"I think we are starting in the wrong place. We need to call Pete and have him ask Momo and Bear if either one of them recognized the name James Withers or Ted Stone.

"I know that look, Sky," Casey frowned, "you think Momo and his sons might somehow, be connected to the Ted Stone-Wither's mystery too?"

"I don't know."

Nelson returned, tucking in his shirt, "Well?"

"It's getting late and you need to get back to work." Dolan and I threw a couple of dollars on the table and left.

He seemed surprised, "If you need anything, I'll be in my office all day tomorrow."

I checked my watch. It was just after four in Honolulu. I called Pete from a pay phone and charged it to my home number but that was a waste of time, he wasn't in the office. I left a message.

Dolan and I went our separate ways. I tried to sleep. My brain was too tired to figure out what was going on. I closed my eyes.

The telephone rang. If that was Dolan, I'd slam the phone back down. How long was I asleep? I looked at my watch and saw it had only been a half hour.

"Hello, Skylar Drake."

"Aloha Drake. It's me, Pete. What's up? I thought you'd be tired of talking to us over here."

"I need you to talk to Momo in the morning." I told him I'd wire a copy of Wither's driver's license with his photograph. The Western Union office was just closing but I convinced the clerk with a twenty.

I went back home around ten and found Dolan was sitting on my front porch drinking a beer. "Couldn't sleep?"

He reached in the paper bag between his legs and handed me a bottle. It was warm, but that's the way he drinks his brew.

I took a long swallow, "I need to get to Withers' hotel."

"Yeah?"

"Right now."

~~~~~~~~~~

The lobby was bustling at midnight, but that wasn't unusual for Hollywood. We took the elevator to the fourth floor. The doors opened, Jack Benny stood in the hall as we stepped out. Dolan froze. "Y-you're..." I grabbed his arm and pulled him down the hall

"Pay attention Dolan." He took a few long breaths and nodded.

I knocked. Nothing. Withers wasn't in. That wasn't unusual for Hollywood either. I took out my lock picks and we were in. Casey stayed by the door to keep watch in case Withers came back. I went into the bedroom to be sure he wasn't passed out or occupied in some embarrassing activity. The bed hadn't been slept in. I opened his closet. He had every color of the rainbow for shirts, neatly hung and several suits and tuxedos. The other closet was full of lady's clothes, nice ones including Hawaiian dresses. He must have a girl living here too. The shoe sizes were rather big for a woman, a tall woman maybe. The dresses were long. He must like them big.

I turned on the ceiling light and scoured the room for anything that could prove out my suspicions. Nothing was in his nightstand but a chrome .32 semiautomatic with pearl grips, a lady's gun. If this guy was really Ted Stone, the choice of gun made sense, maybe. I picked it up with my handkerchief and smelled the barrel. It hadn't been fired recently. Carefully, I put it back and noticed a narrow, gold inlaid wooden box on his dresser. Just as I thought, inside his jewelry was arranged along the bottom with care, and the cuff links were engraved with TES. I called Casey inside, "Bingo! These belong to Ted Stone."

Dolan looked, "Well they're certainly not J.W.W. I think we got it, now hurry and let's get out of here before we get pinched for breaking and entering."

"Watch the door, I'm going to check one more thing."

The desk in the living room was by the floor to ceiling windows with a killer view of the glittering lights of Los Angeles. I opened every drawer and thumbed through every paper. In one I found a receipt from his barber laying on top.

The drawer beneath seemed stuck. I reached in and found three envelopes wedged in the back. All telephone bills. I leafed through them and found Withers made many calls to Hawaii. I aimed the desk light on them and immediately recognized one number, the Honolulu Bureau of the FBI. Many of the others had Moloka'i exchanges.

230

Casey closed the door. "Withers is coming. We have to get out now." He motioned me against the wall by the door. Footsteps in the hallway stopped followed by the jingle of keys. I turned off the lights and joined him. We stood frozen behind the door as it opened. Withers flung the door open, slammed it shut and went directly to the bedroom. He didn't turn on the light or see us in the dark. After we heard the bathroom door close and the shower, we left with the phone bills in hand.

Dolan quietly opened the door to his place. He held his finger to his lips and whispered, "Bev is asleep in the bedroom." We went through the bills at the kitchen table and checked with the operator. They were Moloka'i and Honolulu numbers. Apparently we made too much noise. Bev came out of the bedroom in her robe. Her hair looked like she stuck a finger in a wall outlet. She yawned, "So what's up?" scratching her head.

Without looking up Casey said, "Sorry Bev, can't tell you,"

"Oh, one of those." She bent down, picked up a piece of paper off the floor and gave it to Dolan, "You drop this?"

"Oh, yeah. It's just a barber receipt from a case we're working."

"Oh really? I beg to differ. This is a receipt from my beauty salon. See these initials? The beautician was Mindy and she specializes in wigs." She eyed it closer, "That's a hefty price too. It must have been a long wig.

I dropped the phone bills. "Did you say it was for a

wig?"

"Yeah, and at this price, it was probably a very long one with lots of hair!" She turned around and staggered back to bed.

Dolan whispered, "Why would Ted Stone be masquerading as a woman and Withers?"

My mind immediately went to Wither's bedroom closet. "The long dresses in his closet were lace."

We simultaneously said, "Babs?"

Chapter Thirty

Eight o'clock the next morning we were in Nelson's office, sleep deprived and anxious from all the coffee we drank. He looked over all the information we gave him, "I'll contact the FBI."

We went back to our office, Lory was there.

"Oh good, you're here. I got a call from someone named Pete in Honolulu," and handed us his number.

"You didn't need to come in Lory, not today."

"Oh, I'm fine. I just wanted to get some work done."

We went into my office and called the number. Pete answered. Momo said he didn't know the name either, though he said the photo looked a little like Kai."

It dawned on me, could Withers also be Kai?

Pete hesitated, "Let me take a look... the face looks a little like Chewy, but the license says James Withers."

"Thanks for checking Pete." I hung up and looked at Dolan, "I suspect Ted Stone killed Withers and took his identity. That would mean that James Withers we know is really Ted Stone, and the real Withers may have been Chewy's brother."

"Are you thinking Ted was Babs too?" Dolan sat back in his chair and hit his head on the wall, twice. "And maybe even Kai?"

"What's the connection between Withers, Pete, Ted, Kai, and Babs? And why'd Pete tell us she was his cousin?"

Dolan suggested I call Agents Miller and Tanner in L.A. They weren't in. I left a message.

We heard a big crash from the reception area, "Lory?" We rushed out, Ted Stone had his arm around Lory's throat, holding that little chrome .32 semi-auto to her head. "Hands out where I can see them," he barked.

He'd shaved his beard, lost his glasses and his hair was brown, the color I remember Ted had."

Stone pointed his gun at us. "Get into your office, now!" He shoved Lory through the door and threw her against the wall. "Both guns on the desk!"

"Okay, okay." We did what he said.

"Slide them toward me."

"Is that you Teddy?" leapt out of my mouth. I couldn't help myself.

His head jerked toward me, "Haven't heard that in a while. Move the guns, now."

We pushed them to his end of the large desk.

Lory took a step towards Stone, "Mr. Withers?"

"Get back! I don't want to hurt you but I will," he pointed the gun at her.

She slid down the wall and sat on the floor.

He swung the gun back at us. "I wasn't sure you'd recognize me, Sky. But I guess you did. And you broke into my place, didn't you?" With his free hand he fumbled through the papers on the desk and took the phone bills. "With this heat, by time they smell you two on Monday I'll be long gone."

"Are you related to Otis?" I asked.

"No, Withers is."

"You killed Mr. Withers?" Lory asked.

"Hell no, Withers is alive and well in Honolulu, I believe you know his as Pete."

234

"He's an FBI agent!" Dolan yelled.

"The real Pete Frankel was, but he's dead. Brilliant wasn't it?" He grinned, apparently thinking he was some kind of a genius, "My idea, switching around identities and it almost worked if you people only stuck to your little divorce and cheater business here in L.A."

"Why would you do that?" Lory asked, "Mr. Withers never did anything to you."

"Look, some mob guys from Vegas were after me. I had no choice but to permanently disappear. James Withers hated his father, so he poisoned him and made it look like a heart attack. I took James' place. Good thing the Carringtons hadn't seen him for years."

"What about Frankel?"

"Easy, Pete Frankel and James Withers were friends, but Frankel was a lousy, cheating low-life of an agent. The FBI tried for years to get rid of him. When Pete got his transfer orders for Honolulu, James drove him to the airport and faked car trouble on the way. I came by in a truck, pretended to help and smacked Pete in the head with a jack handle. James took his ID and luggage. I switched his clothes with mine and buried him. I kept my accessories and left fake ones. Hey, my stuff is the real thing!"

"A regular game of musical chairs," Dolan said.

"Why yes, I thought it was rather brilliant."

"So, it was you that took the picture of my dog tags?"

"I guess you don't remember our talks about Korea and our dog tags. I threw mine away, actually I melted them. But you, sentimental fool you are, kept yours. It took me three days to find them in that window seat. I could

235

track your schedule like a Pacific Electric train."

Lory moved, but he spotted her and pointed his gun in her direction, "Don't even think about it, young lady."

He turned back to me, "It wasn't my intention to hurt you Sky, I tried to warn you off, but you got more and more determined. The men I hired for the attack on the boat..."

"One of them bit me in the leg! Where did you find that jerk?"

He sighed, "...and the dog tag picture, both of these would have scared anyone...except you."

"What about those thugs that threw me over the hill, they yours too?"

"Actually no. But I followed you and saw the whole thing. It was a riot."

"You killed Mai Le and ordered the killings of Otis and Rocky."

He sighed again, "As I've previously stated, I really had no choice. Pete told me the boys were coming. Chewy would have spotted me for a fake. As for Mai Le," he shook his head.

"Kai and Babs... Wow." I said.

"Look Ted or whoever you are, turn yourself in, no more killing," Lory pleaded.

"I can't Lory, I can't go to jail. I'd never survive in there."

"What about your sister, Flo?" I asked, "She'd..."

"She's much better off without me. I was a noose around her neck for years. She's free now, and happy. You know she's expecting a baby in a few months..." His face softened. Then as if someone flipped a switch he said,

"Okay enough talking." and raised his gun.

Casey and I hit the floor behind the desk. Casey pulled his spare out of his sock and fired.

The office door flew open shattering the window. "Okay pal, drop the gun unless you want to get perforated." It was Nelson with agents Tanner and Miller. I liked these odds much better. I'm sure Teddy didn't.

Stone backed up, gun still in hand, inching toward Lory. Dolan threw himself on her, distracting Stone. I slid across the desk, grabbed my gun and shot the pistol out of his hand. Thankfully, Nelson and his guys didn't shoot me.

"Stop Stone! Give it up," Nelson shouted.

Ted pulled a switchblade out of his pocket and came at me. A shot from one of the agents missed. I struggled to take the knife from Stone and rolled onto the floor taking him with me. He picked up his gun and shot at Tanner and Miller. Nelson shot back and missed. Ted turned his gun on Casey. I wrapped my legs around his and tripped him as he tried to get up. Miller shot at him again, but he didn't go down. Red spots spread out on to his white shirt where he'd been hit.

"Stop now Stone and you'll live."

Stone eyed the window. He clutched at his belly, blood covered his hand. Ted backed up to the open window.

Lory cried, "He's going to jump!"

I dove over the desk, "Teddy! No!" but he leaned back and, just like that, he was gone. The six of us scrambled to the windows. His body lay face up on the concrete sidewalk... still. As the pool of blood grew around his body, so did the crowd of curious onlookers. His final audience.

<u>Chapter Thirty-One</u>

Captain Nelson called an ambulance. Dolan and I watched the attendants take Agent Tanner downstairs on a stretcher. He'd been shot in the melee but Miller and Nelson were fine. Lory sat in my chair holding a big gauze pad on her bloody nose.

Down at the station Dolan, Lory and I had to fill out those damn statements that come with every shooting. I was glad I didn't work there anymore.

"How did you know to come to my office, Nelson?"

"I got a call from an Agent Jahns in San Diego. She insisted you two were in some kind of grave danger. I called the FBI office in L.A. and got a hold of Tanner and Miller."

"What about Pete, the real James Withers? Dolan asked, "The man murdered his own father and the real Pete Frankel."

"I'll put a call in to the FBI in Honolulu," Nelson answered. "They'll pick him up and ship him back here."

"I'm totally confused." Lory mumbled, "Someone is going to have to explain this whole thing to me again."

After thirty minutes of interviews each, Nelson let us go. I found it hard to believe. "When Robbs was in charge," I said to Dolan. "Everything was accusations and threats." Nelson heard me.

"I told you there was a change in the department. I'm a different than Robbs. You can trust me."

We sent Lory home in a cab while Dolan and I went back to the office and boarded up the broken window in the door. That night we locked ourselves in and turned on the air conditioner. Outside, we heard the clamoring of the press. We had Chinese delivered along with a couple of six packs of beer. Casey and I stayed in the office and waited for the fury to end, staring at the shattered door glass on the floor. The only big piece of glass left said, INVESTIGA on it.

"Guess we need to replace the window," I took a swig of beer.

"Might as well change the name too."

"Yeah, no more Steele Investigative Services. Maybe Drake and Dolan and Associates?"

"Nah, too many letters. You pay by the letter, you know. I like Dolan and Drake better."

I calculated the number of letters in my head. "How about D & D Investigators? Cheaper."

"Sounds good to me."

We tapped our bottles.

THE END

About the Authors

Will Zeilinger and Janet Elizabeth Lynn are husband and wife. They live in Southern California.

Janet Elizabeth Lynn was born in Queens, New York, but escaped the freezing winters and hurricanes for the warmth and casual lifestyle of Southern California.

Ms. Lynn has traveled to the far reaches of the planet for work and for pleasure, collecting wonderful memories, new found friends and a large basket of shampoo and conditioner samples from hotels. At one time she was an Entertainment Editor for a Southern California newspaper. Janet has written nine mystery novels.

Will Zeilinger has been writing for over twelve years. As a youth he lived overseas with his family. As an adult he traveled the world. He says that finding time to write while life happens is a challenge.

Made in the USA
Charleston, SC
27 July 2016